Lanny Waitsman was born in 1951 in Chicago, IL. He has lived in and around the city most of his life, except for sojourns to Rockford, IL, and Normal, IL while attending college. He has a B. S. in Philosophy from Illinois State University. He currently lives in Evanston, IL, with his female cat Saphira.

He has worked on assembly lines, as a graphic production artist, a graphic designer, a real estate agent, and has retired from twenty years in IT doing desktop support.

He has published a fantasy novel titled *Blade Gavotte*, a science fiction novel *Terrekonos*, and has other novels and many short stories in the works.

To my late parents, Seymore and Bernice, without whom I would not be who I am.

And to my late brother Michael, friend and mentor, who is still in my thoughts.

And last but not least, to my sister Shelley, my brother Barry, and all my relatives and friends who put up with my mild craziness and love me anyway.

Lanny Waitsman

FOOTSTEPS ON OTHER SHORES

AUSTIN MACAULEY PUBLISHERS™

LONDON • CAMBRIDGE • NEW YORK • SHARJAH

Ordering Information
Quantity sales: Special discounts are available on quantity purchases by corporations, associations, and others. For details, contact the publisher at the address below.

Publisher's Cataloging-in-Publication data
Waitsman, Lanny
Footsteps on Other Shores

ISBN 9781647501099 (Paperback)
ISBN 9781647501082 (Hardback)
ISBN 9781647501105 (ePub e-book)

Library of Congress Control Number: 2023922822

www.austinmacauley.com/us

First Published 2024
Austin Macauley Publishers LLC
40 Wall Street, 33rd Floor, Suite 3302
New York, NY 10005
USA

mail-usa@austinmacauley.com
+1 (646) 5125767

To all my fannish friends who at one time or another agreed to read and give me feedback on my writing, once I got around to actually submitting it!

And to the Northwest Suburban Science Fiction and Fantasy Writers Group for their invaluable feedback on my writing.

Table of Contents

Castle Erewhon

Lanto remembered his first trip through the Door as if it had been yesterday. It had been five years ago, on his thirteenth birthday. He'd entered the Court Chamber through the formal door as this was a special occasion. His father, King Karl, looked at him with no expression, but Lanto could see the twinkle in his eyes.

"Prince Lanto Sanreal, second of that name, approach the throne!" the voice of Chamberlain Constantis thundered.

Lanto moved forward with a measured step as he had been taught. When he caught sight of his cousin Charisse, he almost missed a step. She was a distant cousin, but they'd spent many years playing and learning their lessons together until Lanto turned eleven. She'd grown into a pretty young girl, looking beautiful in a formal satin gown of light green that complemented her blue eyes and dark brown hair. He wondered if she still played nurse with her dolls and her pet dogs, then reminded himself to keep moving forward.

He managed to keep moving forward with a slight pause that only his father and Charisse had caught. Keeping his eyes resolutely forward and fixed on his father, Lanto reached the base of the seven steps to the throne, and knelt on one knee as protocol demanded.

Lanto saluted, open right hand to his chest, then rose smoothly, looking up at his father. From this close, he could see not only the twinkle in King Karl's eyes, but the twitch of his mouth as he tried to keep from smiling at his youngest son.

"Rise!" King Karl's voice rang out, not as deep and sonorous as the Chamberlain's, but still carrying to the whole hall.

Chamberlain Ross Constantis approached the king's dais and mounted the steps.

He handed the King a shiny bronze belt. It was about three inches wide, but the buckle! It was a rhombus, about seven inches wide and four inches tall, slightly rounded at the vertices. What one could not see when looking directly at the belt was the thickness of the belt and buckle. The band of the belt was two inches thick, with the fastening about three inches thick.

The front of the belt was covered in an intricate design of many colors: gold, silver, blue, and green. As he tried to examine the patterns, he became a little dizzy and even nauseous. Lanto looked away for a moment and the feeling passed.

"Approach the throne!" the Chamberlain's voice rang out again. A small hand signal from the King caused the man to step to the King's right and behind the throne.

Lanto faced his father. Speaking in a whisper that did not carry, even to the Chamberlain, the King asked, "Nervous?"

"Yes," Lanto replied the same way.

"Don't be," came the answer. "We've rehearsed this too many times." Lanto could see the smile that didn't reach his father's lips and relaxed.

"Prince Lanto has reached thirteen years of age today! In honor of this special day, we are gratning him the title "Duke of the Old City" and present him with the Ducal Scepter that belonged to the first Lanto! And in commemoration of that event, we have a special present for the prince."

The Chamberlain stepped directly behind the throne, picked something up and came forward again, holding a carrier from which emerged a mewing sound.

"A cat?" Lanto was a little disappointed. He'd had cats before and liked them. But what was so special about another cat? King Karl could almost have been reading his mind.

"Open it," he directed.

Lanto took the carrier, set it down and opened it. Inside was a long-haired calico cat. It opened its green eyes and looked at him.

"She's beautiful!" Lanto looked at his father, eyes alight with pleasure. But what was so special about another cat? King Karl could have been reading his mind.

"Her name is Satsuma. We will talk later, but for now…"

Lanto took the hint and put Satsuma back in the carrier and the Chamberlain took it from him. It was heavy, but the Chamberlain made light of the burden. Lanto knew exactly how strong the man was. Many who'd thought such a man weak had learned otherwise the hard way.

Lanto turned and walked back down the dais, holding the Ducal Scepter in the crook of his left arm. At the bottom, he turned and saluted one last time, then turned, and walked with the same measured step across the room and out the main door as the entire court saluted him and applauded. He was now able to see his cousin and appreciate how pretty she was. He found himself hoping she'd forgiven him for the pranks he'd pulled on her, like the time he'd dumped a full bottle of yellow paint on her hair. She'd had to get it almost all cut off!

She nodded and winked at him, and it took almost more self-control than he had to not blush. But he could see that somehow, she knew how much pleasure he'd gotten and did a fair blush herself, glancing away to make a remark to her mother. Lanto promised himself that he would talk to her later. For now, back to his rooms and make better friends with Satsuma.

As he departed the Throne Room, the Chamberlain met him with Satsuma's carrier.

"You'd better let the guard carry her for now," he said, handing the carrier to a waiting guard. "Now come with me, the King wants a private word with you."

"As it was written, Lanto," the King said, "you will take your first trip through the Door today."

"The Door? What door?" Lanto asked as he accepted the Belt and put it on. Oddly, it hardly needed any adjustment to fit properly.

"You will need the Belt to go through the Door," King Karl said. "But otherwise you must keep the Belt hidden and never speak of your trips through the Door, except to me or the Chamberlain."

Lanto had asked why not, but his father had not been able to tell him, so he just accepted it and done as he'd been told.

Lanto smiled at the memory. Since then, he had gone through the Door twice a year; on his birthday and exactly six months later. And Satsuma was his faithful companion through all the adventures. Their bond had become so close it seemed as if they could read each other's mind. Lanto was sure it wasn't that, but instead a close empathic bond.

He had learned many things, only some of which could be thought of as learning how to rule. Yet he would never become king, not with three brothers ahead of him! Still, for all the times he'd asked, his father and the Chamberlain never explained to him why he was being trained this way.

The last time he had asked was three months ago. King Karl had been struck down with a virulent fever that only affected him. As he lay dying, Lanto asked one last time.

"I cannot tell you," King Karl replied. "But I can say you will come to understand, and I ask your forgiveness now for not telling you."

Lanto had bowed his head saying, "Of course I forgive you! I know that you never do anything without good reason. I love you and so I will wait."

That was the last time Lanto spoke to his father the King, who passed three days later. Lanto did not cry in public, but when Charisse came to visit him that night, he could not help himself and the tears flowed unbidden.

"Oh, Lanto!" Charisse found herself moved by the sight. She sat on the couch in his suite and held out her arms. Lanto almost fell into them.

"Shh, it's alright," she whispered and tears fell from her own eyes. She held Lanto and rocked him until their tears stopped flowing.

Charisse dried his face with her kerchief and kissed him once on each eye, then on his lips. While they had grown very close over the years and often kissed, this time was different. An almost electric tingle went through their bodies and the kiss became deeper and more passionate.

"Lanto," she started to say, but he kissed her again, answering the question that they both knew she had been about to ask.

When they finally broke the embrace, it was because Satsuma had butted her way between them. She settled down on Charisse's lap, purring like a miniature thunderstorm. Lanto looked at the cat in surprise. He knew Satsuma liked Charisse, but this was the first time she had shown such unconditional acceptance!

Charisse whispered, "I wish we could go through the Door together."

"What? How do you know about the Door?"

Charisse put her hand over her mouth, realizing she had broken her promise to King Karl.

"I wasn't supposed to tell you! Don't say anything, please!"

Lanto couldn't bring himself to refuse, "I won't. But how long have you been using the Door?"

"Oh, I started going through it when you did," she replied, then paused, frowning. "That's odd! I never really thought of it before, but I always go through the Door on my birthday and six months later, the same way you do. I wonder why?"

Lanto frowned, "I can't imagine. But I do know that my father never did anything without good reason!"

Comparing stories, they found that each of them had similar experiences. When they went through the door, they found themselves in a time, place, and body not their own. They always fit right in to the situation as if they had been born into it.

At first, the experiences were situations where they gained skills or knowledge they never had before. But as time went on, the experiences changed. Lanto, for instance, learned many of the crafts of the people in the Old Town, as did Charisse, but sometimes he found himself in the military, starting from infantry and moving up through the officer ranks.

Charisse, meantime, had learned many of the women's crafts, eventually being put in positions of household management. And, oddly enough, in the last two years, they both found themselves in positions of political influence.

Then a reason for the trips through the Door became evident. Rather than floundering politically when having to govern, the training stood him in good stead. Lanto did make the occasional mistake, but not often.

And the military training, in addition to his own martial arts training, helped him the few times he was attacked by irate citizens or the occasional assassin. In times of battle, luckily few, he always led his men personally. He'd found that it inspired them to see him taking the same chances they were. Officers serving under him who wanted to lead from behind were demoted or dismissed.

As Lanto and Charisse talked, neither of them could figure out if the places they went were real or not.

"But they must be real," Charisse exclaimed. "Look at this scar," she continued, pointing to a round mark on her right shoulder. "I was tending a pot of soup and got distracted. It boiled hard enough to throw a scalding hot piece of carrot that hit me right there."

Lanto did his best not to laugh, but something must have showed on his face, for Charisse grabbed a cushion and threw it at him. He tried to duck out of the way, but it still struck him a glancing blow on the left side of his head.

He straightened up. She stood, hands on hips, glaring at him. The sight of her, flushed and scowling made Lanto hold up his hands, palms toward her.

"You may be right," he admitted. "I once took a lance through the meat of my calf," he said, pointing to a round scar on his left leg. "Like you, it healed, but the scar is still there. And once, Satsuma ate some kind of animal. I never was able to figure out what she ate, but about a half-hour after we came back, she threw up bits of fur and bone!"

Charisse bit her lip for a moment.

"And how long do your adventures last?" she asked.

"Odd you should ask. I was just thinking about that. Each adventure lasted a different amount of time. The shortest was three days, but one seemed to last three years! But no matter how long the adventure lasted, it always seemed that I returned the day after I went through the Door."

Charisse gasped, "And I! One day, no matter how long I seemed to be gone."

The relationship between Charisse and himself had grown to the point where, unknown to them, all the court were waiting for the engagement to be announced. And later that day, King Kurt, Lanto's eldest brother who had taken the throne, called Lanto into his private chambers.

"So when are you going to announce the engagement?" the King asked with a raised eyebrow.

Lanto, caught by surprise, blushed.

"Is it that obvious?" he asked.

"Well, maybe not to the blind beggar who lives at the castle gates, but to everyone else, yes."

"We had thought to announce after our next trips through the Door."

"Oh, she told you? She wasn't to let you know about that just yet."

To Lanto's surprise, the King frowned.

"Is there are problem?" Lanto asked.

"Just your brother Harle."

"Yes, Charisse told me that he had approached her. And even though she made it clear she will have nothing to do with him, he still persists. If he weren't my brother, I'd have called him out already," Lanto replied.

"I understand. Don't even think about that. I'll talk to him. If necessary, I'll order him to leave her alone," the King told him. "In the meantime, prepare for your last trip through the Door. It's what, five days away?"

Lanto laughed, "Like you don't know when my birthday is? Yes, it is. May I have leave to move Charisse into the apartments next to mine?"

King Kurt looked at Lanto. He knew that Lanto would not take advantage of the situation, but worried about how it would appear to the court.

"Only if you announce your engagement."

Lanto smiled, "I'll talk to Charisse later today. If she agrees, we will make the announcement at Evening Court."

"Excellent idea!" the King agreed. "Send a messenger with word."

At this Satsuma, riding on his shoulder as usual, set up a thunderous purring.

"See?" King Kurt said. "Even Satsuma thinks it's a good idea!"

Lanto laughed, scratching the cat's head, and bowed himself out of the suite.

And that evening, after a short but intimate conversation with Charisse, followed by the delivery of a short note to King Kurt, the engagement of Lady Charisse Donlon and Prince Lanto Sanreal was announced at Evening Court. The applause, cheers, and well-wishes of the court were almost deafening.

Lanto and Charisse were surprised. Neither of them knew they were so popular in the court, and Lanto, at least, had no idea why. And many variations of the phrase, "What took you so long?" were heard by the couple as they stood in a reception line.

The only person that was unhappy was Lanto's next older brother, Harle.

Harle had made it known to Charisse that he wanted her, but Charisse had spurned him when it became obvious that he did not love her, but only wanted her because of her beauty and position. Unlike other men of the same stripe, Harle did not leave her alone, but kept pressing his suit to the point that she avoided him altogether or only appeared with Lanto.

Harle appeared to be younger than Lanto. But for those who knew both, they soon realized that Lanto appeared older because he was more self-controlled and responsible than Harle. And Harle's resentment stemmed from his inability to control his impulses. Harle's only partners were using him to get into the court. That didn't bother him; they were just using each other. Harle could understand that.

And to cap it all off, only Lanto and, unbeknownst to Harle, Charisse, were allowed to make the trip through the Door. Harle had only heard about the Door by accident. But he couldn't get his hands on Lanto's belt because he never took it off or laid it aside anywhere that Harle had access to. Not to mention that cat of his!

The single time Lanto had laid it aside and left the room, Satsuma had been laying on it. When Harle snuck in and approached her and the Belt, she had hissed at him, then slashed the back of his hand when he tried to take it anyway. It had taken a week for the wounds to heal, and he had to pass it off as a fight with his current woman.

But one secret he had managed to ferret out; King Kurt had a book that was always kept under lock and key in a secure chest in the King's private apartments and guarded by the King's most dedicated soldiers. Only six soldiers, the Chamberlain and the King knew where the chest was, and only the chamberlain and the King had keys to open the chest.

But Harle had managed to get one of the soldiers drunk while off-duty and slipped him a drug that made him tell his deepest secrets, then forget that he had done so.

Most of the secrets were harmless, but two were worth listening to all the rest of the man's drivel. One was a sexual peccadillo that would have ruined the man's military career, if not exiled completely; the other was the existence of the book.

"What's in the book?" Harle demanded.

"Don't know. Only seen it once, and never saw it opened. But the chamberlain and the King seem to know. And I did once hear them saying it concerned Prince Lanto."

Unable to get anything more of use out of the man, Harle bought him more to drink and left the tavern. He had originally thought to have the soldier killed but realized he now had at least a small chance to get access to the book. Harle grinned. Blackmail could be a most useful tool to open doors otherwise locked.

Everything came to a head on Lanto's eighteenth birthday. King Kurt summoned Lanto and Charisse to his private audience room and announced, much to their surprise, that they would be going through the Door together! When they had recovered from the shock, Lanto spoke.

"But why? It's never been done before!"

"I can't tell you just now, but I can say that our father wanted it that way and was able to convince me that it *must* be done that way. Once you have gone through the Door, you will have something with you that will explain everything," King Kurt replied.

"Can't you even give us a hint?" Charisse pleaded. "We might be stepping into danger!"

"All I can tell you is that you must do this, and that you will survive. More than that you will learn after you pass through," the King told them.

The couple looked at each other, then turned back to the King.

"As you wish, so shall it be done," Lanto replied formally.

The expression on the King's face softened.

"I really can't tell you anything else. I truly wish I could, but I don't even understand it myself. And I apologize for that."

Charisse spoke up, "I wish you could, too, but if both you and King Karl were convinced that it must be done this way, of course we will."

The King smiled at them, "You two really are a good match. I wish you the best on your passage."

Then he surprised them both by standing and giving each of them a hug, "Now go and prepare. You only have two hours left!"

After they had departed, Lanto turned to Charisse, "Did that strike you as odd?"

"You mean about going through the Door together?"

"Well, yes, but also the way he wished us well and hugged us. It felt like he was trying to say goodbye!"

Charisse's eyes widened in surprise, "You're right! What could that have been about?"

She started to turn back to the King's room, but Lanto stopped her.

"He won't tell us anything more. And he, like my father, would have if it were necessary. Let's just finish our preparations."

But while this was happening, Harle had not been idle. He'd called the guard to his room and told him what he must do. At first, the guard sneered at him, but when Harle said a few words about the guard's secrets, the guard went white.

Killing Harle was out of the question, but neither could he ignore the request. Caught between the possibility of shaming and exile or following Harle's orders, he could only agree to Harle's request.

Harle then took a bottle of his brother Jason's favorite wine, spiked with a potion that would cause him to die of an apparent heart attack within three days. Taking the antidote, he went to Jason's quarters and shared a glass in honor of the momentous day.

Leaving, he went back to his own suite, where he found a messenger summoning him to King Kurt's rooms. Perfect! Harle was certain that the King wanted him to make amends for the way he had been treating Charisse. As he entered, with another poisoned bottle of wine, this one similar but faster acting, he signaled the guard. And just after he entered, he heard a soft grunt and the sound of a body slumping to the floor.

But when he entered, the chamberlain was there with the King!

"Hail, my King! Greetings, Chamberlain. Before we discuss what I'm sure are weighty matters, may we toast this auspicious day?"

Harle presented the bottle of wine and let the chamberlain inspect it. He knew the man would find no marks of tampering; Harle had been careful to introduce the poison just before the actual corking of the bottle. Still, the chamberlain, after checking and pouring two glasses, made sure that Harle drank before the King.

But Harle's plans had been laid well in advance. He'd fostered the impression that he was not very good at planning, hoping that this day would come. As the King tossed his head back to drink, Harle stepped next to the Chamberlain, slipped out a hidden dagger and stabbed him in the back.

But the chamberlain, still suspicious, had turned and the dagger blow was not fatal. Harle called for his tame guard and the man burst in. King Kurt jumped up and drawing his blade, attacked the man. And the chamberlain swung around with surprising strength, striking Harle empty-handed and knocking him out.

When Harle came to his senses, he saw the King laying lifeless on the couch with a dagger to his heart, and the guard dying, his throat cut and pumping blood in copious amounts. At least that part had worked well!

Calling for more guards, he looked around the room and saw a small chest lying on the floor beneath a picture of Queen Guinefre. But it was open and empty, and the Chamberlain was gone!

Lanto and Charisse were waiting to go through the Door and chatting nervously with each other when they heard a strange sound. Satsuma stood on her pad and hissed as the chamber door opened. They saw the Chamberlain lurch through it, something clasped in one arm and the other bracing himself up against the wall. Charisse exclaimed as she saw the blood running down the man's left leg.

Both of them leapt forward to grab him.

"What happened?" Lanto asked.

Chamberlain Constantis ignored the question, thrusting a large bound book into Lanto's hands. As he slumped against the wall, Charisse ran experienced hands over him, finally finding the knife still sticking out of his back. She tore lengths of fabric from her underskirt, folding one into a pad to staunch the bleeding, and another to bind it in place when she removed the blade. Finally, the Chamberlain spoke.

"Harle!"

Lanto's face hardened, "He stabbed you?"

"Yes. King Kurt is dead, and the guard who did it is probably dead by now too," he gasped.

When Lanto put his hand on his sword and moved to stand up, the Chamberlain grasped at him with desperate strength.

"No. You must go through the Door! The book explains everything."

Lanto looked at the Book in his arms, flipped it open to the first page, and almost dropped it from shock.

Charisse looked at him, "What is it?"

Instead of replying, he handed her the open book. She also gasped in surprise. The handwriting was recognizably Lanto's, and the opening line said, "Listen to him! You *must* go through the Door!"

Lanto and Charisse looked at the Chamberlain.

"How long have you had this?" Lanto asked.

"I saw it first when I was appointed Chamberlain," he replied. "We think it came to us from the first Lanto. I've read some of it. I won't say anymore just now."

"But what will you do?" Charisse asked.

Chamberlain Constantis did something Lanto and Charisse had never seen before. He smiled! It was the most genuine, caring smile either of them had seen.

"That's not your concern. I will do what is necessary, as should you. You should go through the Door now. That's necessary. After you've gone through, you may do as you like, but I recommend you read the first chapter of the Book as soon as you can."

"But what about Harle?" Lanto asked. "He's killed Kurt, or had a hand in it, and who knows what he's done to Jason?"

"Again, not your concern. I have my own organization in place, and if Harle is indeed responsible for your brother's and maybe your father's death, to say nothing of Jason, he will die."

"But that leaves me next in line for the throne!" Lanto said. "I can't leave!"

"Yes, you can," Charisse spoke up. "How many nephews, nieces and cousins do you have that think they want the throne?"

Now the chamberlain laughed, "She's right. There is no lack of people who think they want the throne. And I will be there, or one of my trusted advisors will be, to make sure they learn what's needed. Now enough. Go through the Door and leave the rest to me. Charisse's binding of my wound will keep me going until I reach my second and get to a Healer. So, no more talking. Go now!"

They stood and looked at each other. Then, as if rehearsed, Lanto and Charisse bowed to him. Then they all turned and went their separate ways. Lanto resisted the urge to look back.

He and Charisse approached the Door, Satsuma riding easily on her pad, and paused. Somehow, it looked different. Then Charisse looked up and gasped in surprise. Lanto looked up. Above the door was a carving of two crowns, one a king's crown and the other a queen's diadem and between the two, a stylized cat face! They looked at each other in amazement, then turned back to the Door, clasped hands, and stepped through.

Lanto and Charisse found themselves in a room, clearly some kind of office, that Lanto found oddly familiar. When Satsuma glided over to a perch that was clearly made for her, the sense of familiarity deepened. As he turned to Charisse to tell her, the door opened, and a tall, thin man in the uniform of the city guard entered.

"Captain Sanreal! When did you get back?" the man said.

"Just now, Sergeant Grane," he replied startled. He had spent over a year commanding the city guard during his last trip through the Door. Mastering himself, he said, "May I introduce my betrothed, Lady Charisse Donlon."

The smile on Sergeant Grane's face could have lit a castle ballroom, but he confined himself to a bow to both of them and a hearty, "Congratulations!" He then turned to Satsuma and bowed to her also.

"Hello, Lady Satsuma," he said to her. She yawned, stretched, then purred.

"So now that you're back with your betrothed, you clearly need different quarters. I will arrange that. In the meantime, I suggest you find something to eat, as we just finished the noon meal. Should I have the cook prepare something?"

Lanto smiled. He'd forgotten how prepared the man was for any eventuality.

"No, we'll just take a walk and I can show the Lady the sights. We will find something to eat on the way," he replied.

"As you wish. I will have suitable quarters prepared by an hour before supper. Will you be eating with the men, or do you wish to take supper with the officers?"

Lanto looked at Charisse. She looked back at him with the tiniest of shrugs.

"I will inform you of that later. In the meantime, please have one of the officers' wives or a court lady ready to take care of Lady Donlon."

Sergeant Grane gave him one of his "you really needed to tell me that?" looks, saluted, and left the room.

"Let's take a walk," Lanto said, taking her hand. She wanted to ask what was going on but could see that he was in one of his "don't ask" moods, so she just smiled and followed him out.

As they walked out of the building, Charisse was also struck by a sense of familiarity. The hallways and layout of the rooms convinced her she'd been here before, but she couldn't yet identify the building. They went out through a large atrium and when they went through the door into the street, she *knew* she'd been here during a trip through the Door.

Lanto turned her around so she could see the building they'd just left and she gasped.

"Isn't this—"

"Yes, it's the council hall," Lanto said.

"But it's new!"

"Not exactly. It's only about ten years old, not over two hundred," he told her.

"But that means…" she turned to the north. Where the castle should have been was just a large tract of prairie, "Are we really two hundred years in the past?"

Lanto shrugged, "I don't really know, but it looks that way. Have you been in this time before?"

"Yes, I think so. Let's see, that would mean…"

Just then, a corporal from the city guard ran up to them and saluted.

"Your pardon, Captain Sanreal! Sergeant Grane says he's arranged for your new quarters. I'm to guide you if you're ready."

Lanto returned the salute, "Not just yet. Corporal Hanks, isn't it?"

The smile on the young man's face told Lanto he'd remembered correctly. Lanto then introduced him to Charisse.

The corporal clearly wanted to salute her, but wasn't sure, so contented himself with a bow, "Your pardon, lady, but none of the officers' wives are available to assist you just now."

"That's alright," she said to him smiling, which brought a blush to the young man's face. "Wait, do you know the Lady Gina Rouget?"

The corporal gulped visibly, "I do, my lady! One of her maids is my…" he paused, clearly at a loss for the right word. Charisse could tell that he had wanted to say girlfriend, but clearly, he'd not asked her yet.

"Get word to your friend and have her tell her mistress that Lady Donlon is back from her travels and would like to meet her at," she paused to think, "the Golden Chalice. And," she said as he turned to go, "tell your friend how much you like her. If she likes you even half as much as you appear to like her, I think you'll be happy with her response."

Flabbergasted, he actually saluted her, then dropped his hand, and ran off. Charisse smiled after him, then turned to Lanto.

"She was my best friend while I served at the Mayor's mansion. She will help me with anything I need."

Lanto smiled at her, then suddenly realized he was still holding the Book. Charisse looked, too, then said, "We should find a place to sit and read that."

He grinned, took her hand, and led her two blocks north and one block west to the Golden Chalice, a small pub with good ale and food and comfortable chairs and tables. They sat at a small table and ordered food and drinks.

Lanto pulled out the Book and opened it. As he did, he noticed that it looked newer. After the first lines, they read, "It's good to know you got this and have gone through the Door. I never did find a way to learn what happened to the Chamberlain. But he was right. He would not be the man we know if he had not been capable of handling Harle. So think no more of it."

"All of what I have written is probably gone, since you haven't written it yet. And that's good. You shouldn't know what will happen. We wouldn't want to spoil the surprises!"

At this, they both laughed. It sounded so much like Lanto himself speaking that now neither of them believed it was anyone else.

"The only thing I have left to tell you is this. Yes, you are two hundred years in the past. Live like that's true whether it is or not. Everything you do and learn, you should write in here. I believe it will be of immense value to you and those who follow after. Oh, yes, one other thing; why not get married today? There's nothing to stop you, after all!"

The words ended. The rest of the book was blank.

"He's, I'm right you know. There's nothing to stop us," Lanto said to Charisse.

"There is one thing," Charisse said.

It took a moment before Lanto took her meaning. He knelt on one knee.

"Lady Charisse Donlon, will you do me the honor of becoming my wife?"

"Yes—especially since you asked so nicely," she replied.

They kissed.

At that, the door opened and a tall, willowy brunette in a green dress came in, looked around, and spotted Charisse and Lanto, still in a passionate embrace. She looked at their faces and nodded.

"So, would the evening meal be a good time for your wedding? I can have everything ready by then."

Charisse laughed. "Yes, the evening meal would be fine. We'll have to tell Sergeant Grane to change the rooms he was going to get for us," she said turning to Lanto.

"Done," Lady Rouget said. "I'll send him a message to make sure Lady Satsuma is transferred to my townhouse just over by the council hall. I don't really use it anymore, so you can do with it what you like."

"By the way, are you planning to stay in the military?" she continued, turning to Lanto. "I hear you're a very good administrator, and Mayor Taly isn't getting any younger."

For a moment, Lanto was thunderstruck as he remembered that the first Lanto had indeed left the military to become Mayor of the Old City and from there eventually became King Lanto.

"I'll certainly give it some thought," he replied. With those words, he realized that this was not the end, but truly just the beginning.

Dragon Redux

Steven Lynn had always loved dragons. I suppose it was his uncle Glenn's fault; Steven grew up watching his parents and friends gather together at their dining room table about every two months, playing Dungeons and Dragons from afternoon until late night.

Once Steven was old enough, he joined in playing with his mom, dad, and uncle, then later started playing more often with his own friends. But even though everyone said dragons were myths, he knew in his heart that they were real. After all, didn't every culture he'd ever heard of have some kind of story about dragons?

As he grew older and went to college, this obsession led to his major and minor; he majored in biology with specialization in herpetology and minored in literature. It escaped most people's notice (except his uncle) that he studied mostly literature about dragons. Since he and his uncle shared a birthday, Glenn never said anything about his nephew's choice of research, except to tell him about legends and cultures Steven hadn't found yet.

When he tried to write his doctoral thesis on the possible morphology and evolution of dragons, his advisor gently but firmly steered him away from such a topic, explaining that he'd never get a degree that way. So instead, Steven did work on the evolution of flying reptiles into birds. But Glenn was the only one he allowed to see the additional pages he had written, showing how an alternate evolutionary path would have produced dragons.

After graduation, Steven worked many paleontological digs, always looking for evidence of dragons, although he hid that from his professor and colleagues. Between digs, he haunted used and antiquarian bookstores, looking for anything about dragons.

Oddly enough, Steven was back in his hometown, when he noticed a bookstore he'd never seen before, one specializing in antiquarian and occult books. While he normally did not enter such stores, something drew him up the seven steps. "Why seven?" he wondered idly and into the dim shop. Aside from the elderly proprietor, there was only one other person who was in the shop, a young woman who looked oddly familiar.

"I'm looking for books about dragons," he said, addressing the little old man.

The young lady looked around at him with a startled expression, but he didn't notice as the proprietor said, "Ah, there you are, Mr. Lynn! I'd almost given up waiting for you."

"What? Waiting for me? What are you talking about?"

"Never mind. I have what you're looking for," and with that, the proprietor went into a back room and came out a moment later with an old, hand bound folio. "Take this, Steven. It will explain everything."

Steven looked from the proprietor to the book and back again, "Explain what? And how did you know my name?"

"From your description. 'Just less than six feet, hair too dark to be blonde, but too light to be brown, slightly protuberant teeth, but a good-looking lad, nonetheless, although, he won't think so'," the proprietor said, smiling.

Steven flushed, while the young lady smiled. He caught the motion out of the corner of his eye and turned quickly to look at her. It was her turn to flush and she looked away, although she turned back and moved closer as soon as he turned back to the proprietor.

"But who gave you that information?"

The proprietor set down the book and turned it to him, opening the book. On the inside front cover, hand written, was the description and below, a poem.

"A young man named Steven Lynn

Loved dragons so much it was nearly a sin.

He looked, and he searched

'til he nearly burst,

and he finally achieved his desire.'

"What? That looks like a limerick, but it doesn't even rhyme! And this book!" he flipped to the title page. "This was written in...1776? How can that be? That was over 240 years ago!"

"When he gave it to me, he just told me that you would come for it one day. And here you are."

"But that would make you over 260 years old! Impossible. And who gave it to you? You're just trying to make a sale! Do you think I'm that gullible?"

He turned away in disgust and anger as the proprietor reached out to grab his sleeve. Steven shook him off and stalked out of the store.

Behind him, the young lady stepped up to the counter and started talking to the proprietor.

Steven stalked angrily for a couple of blocks down the street to a local pub, ordered a Guinness, then sat outside to enjoy the summer day. Moments later, the book hit the table in front of him with a thud, and a voice said, "Stubborn and foolish, aren't you?"

Startled, he looked up into the hazel eyes of the young woman who stood there. As he looked at her, it came to him that he'd seen her in other bookstores he'd visited.

"I know you! You've been in some of the same bookstores I've been in. You're not following me, are you?"

She looked disgusted, "Follow you? Maybe you've been following me! And buying the books I've wanted!"

"Books you've wanted? Are you looking for dragon legends too?"

"Give the man a cigar for a good guess! You have a keen sense of the obvious, don't you?" she said. "If you don't want the book, I'll be happy to walk away with it. Twenty-five dollars was a decent price, although I think that old man would have given it to you for nothing."

"Wait! Maybe I was hasty, but you must admit that was a little strange…" he replied.

"No, strange was you not even considering looking at the book and just writing him off. If you'd stopped for a second, you'd have seen this could not be a recent copy or even a halfway decent forgery."

He picked up the book, opened it, and looked more closely. She was right! Experience with many old books over the years had given him the ability to spot genuine from even good fakes, at least most of the time. And this one! He was sorry she'd been so mad that she'd dropped it like she had.

"You're right. I'm sorry! Can I buy you a drink, and we'll look at this together?"

She cooled visibly, then sat down across the table from him, "Is that a Guinness? I'll have one also."

He signaled the waiter for a refill and one more, then turned his attention to the book. As he started turning the pages, he found he kept looking at the young lady. She was slim with a nice figure, dark brown hair, a straight nose a little too large, and a generous mouth. He looked back at the book when she looked at him.

On the title page, just next to the bad limerick, he noticed four lines of script in a language he didn't recognize. He pointed to it.

"Did you notice this?" he said, looking at her.

"Eneile. Eneile Raven."

"*A-nay-la*?" he couldn't quite pronounce it correctly.

"Call me Nell; everyone else does. Only my parents could pronounce it right. Why they chose that name, they never said. And yes, I did see that. It looks something like Latin, but the words aren't right."

They both looked at the inscription, but still could not figure it out. Steven turned to the title page.

"A Natural History of Dragons."

He snickered but cut it off short as Nell glared at him. He started turning the pages.

"This mostly looks like a compendium of all the dragon legends, we already know. Here's St. George's dragon, Fafnir, Grendel…" he kept turning the pages. But as he reached the later pages, he suddenly noticed something between two pages. He started to reach for it, but Nell beat him. She pulled out a folded piece of parchment.

"This looks like a map!"

He studied it.

"That word at the top. Is that—"

"Arizona!" they exclaimed in unison.

They looked at the map and the gulches in the mountainous area, and the cave marked along the rise on one foothill. Steven was struck by a sense of familiarity but couldn't figure out why. As he was thinking, Nell spoke up.

"Isn't this word 'Apache'?"

"That's it!" his fist hit the table with a thud and rattled the mostly empty glasses.

"What's what?"

"From 'A Princess of Mars'! That looks like the description of the area where John Carter found the cave. Could this be the same cave that he found?"

Nell looked at him, amazed.

"What would that have to do with dragons? And wasn't that fiction?"

"How would I know? But I swear that area matches the description of the area where Burroughs had John Carter hide from the Apaches. I'm sure of it!"

Nell looked, but wasn't sure if he was right. She hadn't read the book but once or twice and didn't remember it well enough.

"Let's find that bookstore again. Maybe that bookseller can tell us, or at least, he's got to have a copy of 'A Princess of Mars' handy," Steven said excitedly.

They reached for their glasses in unison, drained them, paid and walked out. But when they reached the address of the bookstore, it wasn't there. A Starbucks was doing a brisk business. Nell and Steven looked at each other, then both looked again at the address. The address was right, but no antiquarian bookstore!

They looked at each other again, turned and went back to the pub. Nell ordered them each another Guinness, but as the waiter turned away, Steven called him back.

"Do you have Tullamore Dew?"

"No, I'm sorry, we don't. Our next shipment won't be until next week."

"How about Beam's Choice?"

"Yes, we have that."

"I'll take a shot." He turned to Nell, "I need something stronger after that!"

Nell turned to the waiter.

"Make that two."

When the drinks came, Steven reached for the shots and handed one to Nell.

"Over the lips and past the gums, watch out stomach, here it comes!" he toasted.

They downed the shots and Steven, looking at Nell's expression, could see her response.

"Smooth!" they said in unison.

"How did you know?" Nell asked, amazed.

"One, because it is. Two, that's the usual post-salute for a shot of Beam's Choice. Something I picked up from my parents and Uncle Glenn."

Nell laughed, "They sound like a great bunch of people."

Steven suddenly found himself attracted to the way she looked, especially when she smiled.

"They are. It's due to them that I have such a great interest in dragons. Ever since I can remember, they used to play Dungeons and Dragons. Somehow, I knew that dragons really existed someplace."

"Sure! They must have. Why else would there be so many legends in all the different literature? As my father used to say, 'Where there's smoke, there's fire!'" they finished in unison. Steven picked up his beer, Nell did likewise. They clinked the glasses together and drank.

*****

When Steven opened his eyes, the morning light was shining in through his apartment windows, and there was a thunderous knocking on his front door.

"Alright, you don't need to smash the door down!" he threw on a robe, and yanked it open, surprising Nell who was standing there with her hand raised to knock again.

"I was knocking normally, not pounding!" she said angrily.

Steven groaned. "Come in," he said. "I'm sorry, it must be my head. How much did we drink last night?!"

Nell looked sympathetic, "If I hadn't had a glass of water by my bed all night, I'd probably be in the same shape. I lost count after the fourth."

"Four? Why didn't you stop me?"

Nell smiled, "You can be very persuasive when you put your mind to it. Speaking of which, when do you want to leave?"

"Leave? What?" he groaned. "You'd better sit down for a moment while I do something so I more resemble a human."

He gestured to the sofa in the living room, then went into the kitchen for a large glass of water, and headed for the bathroom. A glass of cold water down his throat, another splash of cold water on his face, and a hot shower sobered him up some.

He remembered then that they had planned a trip to Arizona to see if they could locate the cave and had planned an early start. As he finished dressing, his mind started to plan what was needed for the trip, including airline tickets, rental car, and camping gear.

"Well, the first thing we'll need is," he started as he walked out of the bathroom, then paused as Nell reached into her bag and pulled out three small folders; two with an airline logo and one with a rental car logo.

"I got them this morning before I came over here."

He slapped his forehead, groaned at the residual pain, then grinned at her. "How about getting more recent maps? I know a professor at Arizona State University who can probably help."

"A geology professor? It wouldn't happen to be Dr. Glen Cameron by any chance?"

"As a matter of fact," his voice trailed off. "How did you know?"

"Same way you did. He's helped me with some of the projects I've worked on."

"I guess we could hardly miss using the same resources," Steven smiled at her.

She smiled back, "It looks that way. I got the tickets for a ten o'clock flight, which puts us in Phoenix at one p.m., but leaves very little time for you to finish getting ready."

"That's no problem."

He ducked into his bedroom, appearing moments later with a duffle bag and backpack, "Let's go!"

Nell looked at him, amazed.

"I've had to leave on a moment's notice so many times that I always have luggage ready for situations like this. All I have to do is grab the right bags for the kind of terrain I'm going to, and I'm ready to go! And you?"

Nell brought her eyebrows back down and said, "Well, I may not be quite as prepared as all that, but I had more time to pack. My stuff is already here."

"So, let's go," he replied.

*****

When they arrived in Phoenix, they picked up the rental car, then went to Arizona State University, where they had arranged a meeting with Dr. Cameron. He looked at the map, then pulled out a sheaf of topographic maps of the state, and helped them locate the site that best matched it. Luckily, it was only a three-hour drive.

"But you'll need a jeep, Range Rover, or a Humvee to drive in that area, or better yet, horses." He told them, "It's the back of nowhere, and extremely rugged, as you can see. And it will make the trip more like six to eight hours."

He made copies of the maps and handed them to Nell.

"Yes, we got a Range Rover already, but the horses are a good point. We're only planning on a three day excursion, but if you don't hear from us by the fifth day, please send a rescue party. We really have no idea what we'll find."

"No problem there." He agreed, "I'd hate to lose the two people who have given me the most interesting extra-curricular assignments I've ever had."

He smiled at both of them.

Steven and Nell thanked him, got in the Range Rover, and left

*****

The next day they arrived in the general area. Steven and Nell left their rental at the ranch where they had hired the horses. They checked the map and supplies and started their ride. After a half hour, he looked at Nell and smiled.

"What?" she said.

"Oh, it's just that suddenly this reminds me of some of the D & D expeditions that Uncle Glenn ran at my parent's house."

Nell laughed.

"I never played myself, but I had lots of friends who did. They used to tell stories of the adventures."

"Yes. I can almost hear my uncle's voice say, 'Your horses head west across scrublands, moving toward the foothills of the mountain range. Roll for randos.'"

He chuckled.

"What are 'randos'?" she asked.

"Oh, that means we have to take a check to see if monsters randomly attacked us. Short for random."

He laughed again, "But don't get me started telling stories. I love them a lot and could go on for hours!"

Nell laughed in response.

"Warning received and understood!"

Steven changed the conversation back to a discussion of their route, how long it would take and plans for camping.

On the second day, Steven stopped suddenly and looked around with the binoculars. He pointed up to a range of hills and said, "That looks like our destination!"

"Right," Nell agreed.

He clucked to the horse and started off. After an hour of riding in bad terrain, they stopped again and looked up.

"Is this it?" Steven asked.

Nell checked the maps and looked around, then pointed to the highland on their left, "That looks like the plateau John Carter mentions. We need to find the pass he was searching for, then find the defile that his horse took. There should be a distinct rock formation on the plateau; to the left should be the trail to the pass, to the right the defile his horse took."

It took another hour to find the pass, but since it was getting to be noon, they stopped for lunch and to rest the horses. Refreshed, they continued on.

"There!" Nell said. "That looks like the rock formation in the story. To the left is the pass, and see the small opening on the right? That should be our defile."

"Great! Let's go!" Steven said, voice betraying his excitement.

They followed the defile, found the trail, and continued on. Since it was wide, but not quite enough for two horses side by side, Steven took the lead. Soon they came to the turn and saw the cave mouth.

They stopped dead, for from their mount's back, they could clearly see a skeleton lying just in front of the cave mouth.

In hushed tones, Steven said, "I always thought Burroughs was just telling a story when he said John Carter had told this to him directly. Maybe he wasn't?" His voice trailed off.

They looked at each other, dismounted, and approached the cave. As the interior of the cave came into view, they both stopped, gasped, and exchanged looks of amazement.

Inside the cave, they saw the skeleton of a man, the mummified remains of a woman, and the line of human skeletons dangling from the roof. They even saw the charcoal burner and copper brazier.

"It's true," Nell gasped.

She started forward, but Steven reached out and drew her back before she could enter the cave. As she turned toward him angrily, he removed his pack, rummaged around, and pulled out two Army issue gas masks.

"Just in case," he said.

Nell's anger at his grabbing of her vanished.

"Oh, yes, the greenish gas. Do you think it's still there?"

"Why chance it?" Steven put his mask on and stooping, entered the cave. Nell did likewise and followed.

Once inside, they pulled out LED flashlights, and looked around. Now they could see what John Carter had not. Inside, the cave opened up into a chamber, almost a hundred feet wide and about seventy-five feet high, but with a mostly level floor. They also saw three ledges about ten or twelve feet above each other, with four openings each. Ramps connected each level.

"Now that's odd," Steven said. "Notice how regularly spaced the openings are?"

"Not only that, those look more like doors than cave mouths," Nell replied. "Let's take a closer look."

As they approached, they could see that they were indeed doors, each one made of different materials ranging from wood to copper, bronze, iron, and even one that seemed to be steel. Each door had pictographs on them, but what startled them the most was the bronze door's pictograph was clearly the outline of a dragon!

Nell reached out to open the door, but Steven stopped her.

"Before you open that, you know how to shoot a rifle?"

She sneered at him, "Better than you! I have a marksman's rating on almost all types."

"Good."

Steven reached back and took off the long case she had seen him sling next to his backpack. When he opened it, Nell saw two Winchester repeating rifles suitable for hunting big game.

"Surely, you don't plan to kill a dragon!"

Steven looked at her as if she was crazy.

"Of course not! But do you have any idea what else we may encounter? If you do, I'm willing to listen."

Nell bent down to look at the rifles, trying to hide her embarrassment.

"Sorry, I should have known better. You're right, we need to be prepared."

They checked the rifles, loaded them, and checked the safeties.

"Ready?" Steven asked.

"Whenever you are."

"Ladies first," Steven replied with a smile.

"Brains before beauty," she grinned back.

Steven gave a bow, then slowly pushed the door open. Beyond it, they saw an oval tunnel with a slight downward slope. Steven stepped in cautiously, but there was no need. There was no-one inside, no openings to be found. He could see no light coming in.

As Nell stepped through, he said, "Wait! Hold the door!"

She grabbed it quickly, but it pulled strongly against her grip, "Hurry!"

Steven grabbed a large rock and jammed it between the door and the jamb. But the rock shattered, and the door closed anyway. No amount of pulling sufficed to open it.

As the stepped back, Nell exclaimed, "Look!"

Steven played his flashlight over the back of the door and saw an inscription, but it was written in the same unknown language he had seen in the book. In frustration, he tore off the gas mask and threw it on the floor. While the air had an odd smell to it, there was no gas to knock him unconscious.

But when he looked again at the inscription, he found he could understand it now.

"It's that same pseudo-Latin," Nell said, her voice still muffled by the gas mask.

"It says, 'The door is sealed 'til the quest is fulfilled. Show the treasure and return at your leisure'. Not very good rhyming, but the meaning is clear. If we find what we seek, we'll be able to return."

Nell looked at him skeptically.

"Do you really believe that? And how did you read it?" she asked.

Steven grimaced, "I don't know. I want to, since this is the only way back, but I'm trying to maintain a healthy skepticism. And I couldn't read it until I took off the mask."

"I see. Well, I'm not going to take off my mask! And since there's nothing else to do, shall we proceed?"

She waved down the tunnel.

As they walked further, the tunnel took several turns until Steven's usually accurate sense of direction was confused. Suddenly, they both felt a wave of weakness pass through them. Nell looked at him, but he just shrugged. He had no idea what was happening.

Finally, the incline began to flatten out, and they started to hear an odd sound. It was a regular, but sibilant sound that grew louder and they began to see light. Soon, they could see a reddish light that waxed and waned in time with the sound, brighter as the sound increased and dimmer as it softened. Also, another steady light that was more yellowish became evident.

The tunnel leveled out and turned to the left. As they made the turn, Steven and Nell stopped in amazement, not really expecting what they saw. The tunnel debouched into a large cave with an opening to the right through which sunlight streamed. But in the middle of the cave!

A huge serpentine form lay, curled around a large mound of jeweled lumps. It shone with all the colors of precious gems, but tended toward red, gold, and bronze, with highlights of pearl and emerald around the eyes and on the chest. Steven's best guess was a total length of about fifty feet; a ten foot length of snout and neck, twenty foot body and twenty foot length of tail.

It was this beautiful dragon that was the source of the sound and light. Asleep, it snored. And on the exhale, a five foot flame flickered out from the slightly open jaws.

As they stared in amazement, a breeze blew in through the opening and swirled around the cave. As it passed them and on around to the dragon, the nostrils (a good two feet across) twitched, opened a little more, and sniffed. One brilliant, red eye opened and peered around, spotting them. The head came up and looked at the two explorers.

"Well, don't just stand there, come in and introduce yourselves," a sibilant hiss came. "I am Galrina. My mate, Golnir, is out hunting at the moment, but I expect him back soon."

Steven, startled, took an involuntary step back, bumping in to Nell. Then he gathered his wits and courage and stepped out into the cave.

"My name is Steven Lynn, and this is my companion, Eneile Raven."

"So, you've finally arrived! We've been waiting for you for quite a while. You certainly took your time, didn't you?" Galrina said.

Nell tugged at his sleeve in the middle of this, "Are you talking to that thing?"

"Why, yes. Don't you hear her?"

"Hear her? I hear a lot of hissing, but that's all. Her?"

"Sure. She says her name is Galrina, and her mate, Golnir, should be back soon." He looked back at Galrina, "Nell says she can't understand you, but I hear you speaking perfect English!"

"What is 'English'?" Galrina asked. "I'm speaking my language; she would understand me if I spoke to her, or maybe she just needs to take that thing off her face."

Galrina's attention switched to Nell.

"So, you can't understand me?" she sounded annoyed.

Nell just stared.

"She thinks you might be able to understand if you take off the gas mask," Steven said.

She looked at him askance, then reached up, took off the mask and breathed cautiously. Her nose twitched, but she just kept breathing, and as nothing happened, relaxed.

"Can you understand me now?" Galrina asked

"Now I understand you a little," Nell said, amazed.

"Galrina said you'll understand her better when she speaks to you, but also thinks you need to listen better."

Nell glared at him.

"Just telling you what she said," Steven told her.

He lifted his hands, palms toward Nell. Suddenly, a blast of hot, dry, sand-laden air shot into the cave.

Galrina shrieked like a high-pitched locomotive whistle as she curled tighter about the lumps, which Steven suspected were eggs, "Golnir! How many times have I told you not to do that!"

A low, rumbling voice said, "Sorry! I'll be more careful, but I heard you talking. What is going on?"

"Steven finally arrived," she replied, pronouncing it "Seeven." "He's brought his mate, Nell."

"She's not—"

A larger, bronze head slowly moved into view from outside, followed by a seventy foot length of male dragon. Looking at them both, Steven now noticed that Galrina had a frill around the back of her huge head, which fanned out behind ears that stood up, while Golnir had a fan of spikes in a similar position. Oddly, their ears reminded him of dog's ears; they stood up from the sides of the head and swiveled in such a way as to make the face expressive, although the lips did not move much.

Golnir's colors were also red and bronze, but the highlights were purple and green.

Steven tried again, "She's not my mate, she's my…"

He stopped and frowned.

"What's wrong? And is that Golnir?" Nell whispered to him.

"Yes, that's Golnir. But there seems to be no way to say friend. There's mate, or sibling, but nothing else." He turned toward the dragons, "Nell is joining me on my search for you, but she is neither mate nor sibling."

Both dragons' eyes widened. Steven could now see pupils like cats, with a nictitating membrane that was flickering over their eyes now as they tried to make sense of this. They looked at each other, then back toward Steven and Nell, and said in unison, "Mate!"

Steven looked at Nell and shrugged, "Okay, mate."

"I'll 'mate' you later," she hissed at him.

Golnir and Galrina made hissing noises with breaks. It took Steven a moment to understand it was dragon laughter.

"What's so funny?" Nell asked, scowling.

"Only mates hiss at each other in that way," Golnir replied.

Even Nell caught that and had to laugh.

"So, you are here for the eggs?" Galrina said. "You may take two from my clutch; Golnir will take two from another clutch."

"We don't want you to steal them! Just ask," Nell said.

"Dragons do not ask. They take from those weaker, or give to those stronger," she replied. "There is no other way."

"She's right," Steven said. "This is the way dragons interact. They are not social animals, like humans are; they've never needed to cooperate at anything, because there is nothing stronger, except another dragon."

"Oh!" Nell said, startled. She looked again at the pair of dragons.

While Steven was explaining, Golnir had left. Moments later, a smaller version of Golnir, only about twenty feet long, crept into the cave.

"Food?" it hissed, looking at Steven and Nell, and starting toward them.

Galrina slapped him across the snout with her tail, not even moving the rest of her body, and said, "Not food!"

She looked at them and said, "Gorolan is but a Youngling, only fifty human years old. He has not been practicing for a short time and sometimes forgets to use full sentences. Or maybe he's just lazy. You may take him with you, so you can learn before the others hatch. But send him back; he has another destiny than staying in your world."

Galrina turned to Gorolan and started to hiss at him. He hissed back, his wings flaring up from his back until she slapped him with her tail again. He settled down but turned to glare at Steven and Nell.

"He does not want to go and does not want to obey. When he does not, hit him with something hard across his snout. He will stop."

"But we can't—" Nell started to say. Steven reached out and stopped her.

"We will. Thank you for the gift."

"No, thank you. Dragons need to explore and colonize new territory, or we will eventually die. Now take these two eggs," she uncoiled a bit and rolled two large leathery eggs, about the size of a medicine ball, toward them. "When they hatch, they need live or freshly killed meat, and lots of water. Keep the eggs warm, like this sand."

Steven approached the sand pile that held the other eggs. About 50 degrees C. he estimated.

"That shouldn't be a problem. How about their speech? And names?"

"Younglings know their names from the moment they hatch. They will probably follow you around after hatching until they reach two months old. At eight months, they will be self-sufficient and will be able to have normal conversations. At ten months, the wings will have developed to the point of being able to fly. And they will starts to flame," she added, looking at them consideringly.

"Flame? You do flame?" Nell asked.

Galrina turned her head toward an alcove of the cave, which they now saw contained an animal carcass, opened her mouth, and belched a ten foot long flame. The backlash of heated air made them both exclaim and duck. Looking back up, they saw Gorolan leap to the carcass and start tearing into the seared meat.

"We need to eat rock which contains the fire element before we can flame, but it can stay in our system for many days before we need to eat more."

Evidently, Nell had been working on listening, for she asked, "Fire element?"

Steven frowned, thought for a while, then suddenly turned to her, and smiled.

"Phosphorus!"

At that moment, Golnir came back, scooted into the cave, and opened his mouth. Two more dragon eggs tumbled out, rolling toward Steven and Nell.

"Gorok and Galah already had twelve in their clutch, so I took two." He said, "Now you must go. Take Gorolan and send him back when the younglings are able to fly. Go quickly, you must not linger."

Steven started to ask why, but suddenly felt another inexplicable wave of weakness. Recovering, he saw Nell had also felt it. He reached into his backpack and pulled out a large canvas bag. It was just large enough to hold the two eggs Galrina had given him. As he was considering what to do, she hissed at Gorolan who stopped eating, came over, and took the remaining eggs in his mouth.

Another wave of weakness washed over them. "Goodbye!" Steven said, "We'll come back another time to visit."

"No! You must not! Go now and never return!" Golnir roared at them, "If you stay, you will die!"

Steven and Nell turned and went back into the tunnel, Gorolan following. As they got halfway back, another wave of weakness, slightly less washed over them. They picked up their pace.

At the door, the inscription blazed brightly, and the door opened. They ran through into the Arizona cave and dropped to the floor. The weakness ebbed and Steven looked at Nell.

"Success!" he grinned weakly.

She smiled back.

"Can we go now?" Gorolan had dropped the eggs and was looking at them.

"Yes."

They got up slowly, the weakness still affecting them, left the cave, and went to the horses. Steven pulled off the saddlebags from his horse, went back in the cave, and gathered up the other two eggs. Coming out, he heard Gorolan hissing at Nell, who said, "We don't have any food for you here!"

Steven looked at Gorolan and said, "Are you old enough to fly?"

Gorolan launched himself into the air with a combined jump and strong downward stroke of his wings, circled them, and landed.

"Then you may hunt for yourself, but never out of your sight of us," Steven told him.

"Good!" Gorolan launched himself again and flew a widening spiral up and out. They almost lost sight of him when he dived, flaming, and landed.

Nell turned to Steven, "Isn't that the direction of the ranch we got these horses from?"

"Yes, I think so. We'd better hurry back!"

As they rode the horses toward Gorolan, he launched himself up again and came back. The horses tried to shy away, but Steven and Nell, both experienced riders, were able to keep them under control, though they danced nervously when Gorolan approached.

"Strange food, but good. Are those food, too?" he asked, looking at the horses. "They look the like my meal just now. But that was smaller and had some king of covering on them, not clean scales."

"No! How many did you eat?" Nell asked, alarmed.

"Just one. Not very hungry now," Gorolan replied.

Steven sighed, "Let's keep an eye on him. Then we'll have to make some kind of arrangement when we return so he's not just eating anything he wants. We don't want to have to pay for horses consumed by him."

He turned to Gorolan and said firmly, "No eating anything you like! When we meet other humans, they aren't food. And you must only eat what I tell you to!"

Gorolan snarled at him, but Nell, who had found a large stout branch from god-knew-where, clouted him on the tip of the snout with it.

"Listen to him. And me, too!" she hissed at him, even managing to sound like Galrina.

Gorolan stared at her but ducked his head in a clear sign of submission. The sight caused Steven to smile, although he hid it quickly as she started to turn her head toward him.

"It looks like we have our work cut out for us. I don't know about you, but I never thought about our success. Now what?" Nell asked.

"Don't know. Well, at least we have a couple of days to figure it out. We'll make camp on the plateau and talk about it tonight and as we return," Steven replied.

After returning the horses and paying the rancher for the loss of one of his sheep, Steven and Nell considered what to do with the dragons. Nell left on some errand, while Steven made some calls, not the least of which was to his uncle Glenn. With his help, Steven was able to buy a ranch with cattle and sheep so food was not an issue. And the dragons were able to understand and speak both dragon and English.

"Nell came back after her errand was complete to spend some time with Steven and train first Gorolan, then his siblings, not to eat any food not provided to them by humans. Steven and Nell did marry before the four dragonets reached maturity and Gorolan went back," Glenn told his great-granddaughter.

"But how did the dragons become our friends, Gampa?"

"That, Stella, is a story for another time."

Habitat

"Station One, report!" Aaron Hawkins barked.

"Station One ready," Matt Arbor replied.

"Station Two, report!"

"Station Two ready," Marcelle Watts confirmed.

"Station Three, report!"

"Station Three ready," Glenn Shandling was calm.

"Station Four, report!"

"Station Four re—" George Treinkman, Station Four commander's voice cut off suddenly.

"Station Four?" Aaron repeated.

The only reply was static.

"Station Three, can you see Station Four? What is their status?"

"Station Four looks—wait a minute!"

Indistinct words sounded in the background. Then Joan Mallert's voice sounded again, "Station Four is out of position! I see a cloud of something around the middle of the fuselage, and their running lights have gone out."

Suddenly, a faint signal came in.

"George Treinkman, Station Four, reporting. We have been hit by a small object, probably a small asteroid. We've lost our propulsion and life support. I have rigged a small repeater from my suit communicator to the main radio. Jack Franken was killed by suit puncture; the asteroid passed through the shoulder of his suit, and we could not patch it in time."

"Are the rest of you okay?" Aaron asked worriedly.

"The rest of us are fine, but we can't maneuver and have no life support!" His voice got ragged, "We need help!"

"Okay, just a moment while we get someone there," Aaron replied. "Station Three, can you reach them?"

"Not before their suit's oxygen supply runs out. With turnover, six hours is the best time we can make."

April Jones, Aaron's second-in-command said, "But there's only four hours of air."

"Couldn't we do a high speed rendezvous?" John Scanlon, the project manager, said.

"It would still take too long. And how do we pick them up?" Aaron replied. "Ballistics is an exact science. We can't get around the laws of inertia!"

"Too bad we can't just lasso them as we fly by. Then we wouldn't have to slow down!" John said. He was a rodeo fan and often practiced lassoing on his vacations.

"Yeah, but the velocity differential would rip them apart," April replied. "If we could just find a way to absorb the shock. It's too bad we couldn't equip the tugs with some kind of lifeboat."

Silence filled the bridge as each person sought a solution. How could they save the three astronauts and salvage the project?

Suddenly, April looked up, "Oxygen tanks!"

Aaron frowned, "What about them?"

John laughed, "Pull out the oxygen tanks from the disabled tug, rope everyone to the tanks with a cable, and open the valve on one. Instant rocket!"

"That reduces the amount of delta v between tug Three and the survivors of tug Four!" April chimed in.

"Okay, but there will still be a fair delta v left. How do we get around that?" John said.

Aaron thought for a moment, then smiled, "Springs!"

It was April and John's turn to be puzzled, "Springs?"

"Attach a cable with a steel plate on one end to a spring on the other, with the spring attached to the tug. Tug Three, as it passes the party, lets out the cable with the plate. The group from Tug Four catches the plate with a strong magnet. The spring absorbs the difference in delta v and gives them enough boost to catch up to the tug!" Aaron smiled again.

John frowned, "That's pretty tricky. Do you think it will work?"

April and Aaron said, "Better than nothing!"

They looked at each other and nodded.

"Base to Tug Four, come in," Aaron called.

"Tug Four here. What have you got?" Jack replied.

Aaron explained the scenario.

"That might work." Jack sounded much happier. "We can take two tanks, and hook to one for the extra oxygen if we need it, or for more propulsion!"

"Tug Three, can you make that work?" Aaron asked.

"Yes! Without having to slow down, we can get to Tug Four in about two hours. Well within the oxygen limits of the suits."

*****

61

"Okay, let's review the mission objectives and specs," Aaron said. He looked around the room. John Scanlon, Project Manager, bald, tall, and thin. April Jones, V.P. of Habitat Production, blond-haired, green-eyed, medium height, and a bit chubby. Matt Arbor, Station One/Tug One Commander, brown hair and eyes, short and fat, but surprisingly strong. Marcelle Watts, Station Two/Tug Two Commander, a bit taller than Matt with red-brown hair and brown eyes. Joan Mallert, Station Three/Tug Three Commander, also brown hair with a bit of grey, green eyes, and slim. George Treinkman, Station Four/Tug Four Commander, light brown hair, gray eyes, short and chunky, completed the group surrounding the table.

"April?"

"Thank you, Aaron. The object of the Habitat Project is to create a colony in space by moving an Apollo-class metallic asteroid, number US531-2025 into near-earth orbit, then convert it into a habitat capable of housing 250,000 people. Project Manager Scanlon will review the details of the conversion. John?"

"Thank you, April. Overall, the process of conversion resembles blowing up a balloon. We started by drilling into the center of the asteroid, using metallic sintering of the rubble to separate out the minerals for use in constructing the rest of the structure and storing gases and water for future use," John explained.

"Then we dig out a large chamber in the middle of the asteroid for holding water. We set up large mirrors to concentrate sunlight and focus it on the asteroid, melting it from the outside in. When the heat converts the water to steam, it expands to inflate the molten metal, cooling it in the process.

"As you can imagine, the calculations for this process were very intricate and precise. The idea is to have a large metal shell of a specific thickness, with air and water in the middle. Then we spin the habitat to create centrifugal force equivalent to one-half gravity at the outer edge."

"Thanks, John," Aaron stood. "Obviously, we would have decreasing levels of gravity toward the center, with zero gravity at the axis of rotation. These reduced levels of gravity can be used for entertainment and medical purposes, to say nothing of the architectural possibilities."

"The problem we now face is the loss of the tug. It leaves us unable to manage the four mirrors. And three mirrors doesn't give us sufficient coverage to complete the mission. Since we have a timetable to keep in order to retain the funding. I'm now opening the floor for discussion. Any ideas?"

George spoke up, "You're sure we can't use three mirrors? Can't we expand the surface area of the three to complete the coverage?"

"Actually, we could if there were no other constraints. But the time constraint keeps us from being able to do that before the deadline for the shell fabrication, since the three-mirror focus does not produce the necessary heat in the time allotted," Aaron pointed out.

"Can we use the sintering chamber? Convert it into a tug and try again?" Joan asked.

"No, it would be the same issue with time," Marcelle said. "How long would it take to adapt the structure from a sintering station to a space tug?"

'Three months," April said, looking up from her terminal.

"Again, too long," Aaron replied. "The deadline for the completion of this phase would be long past before we complete the reconfiguration."

Silence fell. Finally, Matt spoke up.

"Can we get another tug?"

Aaron frowned, "The only other tugs available are owned by Space Solutions Inc. And I don't think Steven would lend us one, even if he consented to talk to us in the first place."

Silence fell in the room. They all knew that Aaron and Steven had been boyhood friends, even sharing the same vision of creating space habitats. None of them knew what had happened, but the former friends had become bitter rivals in the race to create the first successful, sustainable space habitat capable of holding more than five thousand people.

Aaron spoke up, "Any other options you can think of?"

Nobody answered.

"Okay, I guess there's no choice," Aaron said. "April, please put in a call to Space Solutions and see if you can set up an appointment for me to talk to Steven."

*****

Barry Watts was sitting at his desk, writing up the latest status report for Space Solutions when the televisor chimed.

"Answer," he said, not looking up.

"Hello, Barry." He looked up, startled, not having expected to see or hear from his ex-wife, Marcelle, since their agreement to disagree on which kind of orbital habitat to devote their energies.

"What are you doing, calling me here?" he blurted.

"Well, it has been a while since we talked."

"Yes," he said. "But we had an agreement not to call each other at work as I remember."

"We did. But I need to set up a business call with Mr. Samael."

Barry's eyebrows went up again, "Why? Did you change your mind and decide to join us? That's great!"

"Don't jump to conclusions," Marcelle cautioned. "Actually, it's my boss. He needs to talk to Steven."

"What?" he yelped. "They haven't talked to each other for more than five years! I'm not sure that Steve will speak to Aaron for any reason. How come April didn't call? Isn't she the one who should be contacting me?"

"Yes, but she asked me to call you first to be sure we could make contact without problem," she replied. "Can you set up a call for Aaron to talk to Steven?"

"I think so but let me check. I'll call you back in 24 hours. By the way, good to see you again. How's the construction going?"

"Pretty well, but we've run into a problem. That's what Aaron wants to talk to Steven about."

Barry laughed wryly, "Welcome to the club! We were just setting up a mirror to direct the sunlight to our agricultural section when a piece of orbital debris struck just the right, or maybe the wrong, way. It ripped the material along a line that wouldn't allow us to use the remaining piece since it wasn't big enough."

"And we lost a tug to a meteor," Marcelle sighed.

"That's tough. Are you under the same deadline constraints we are?"

"Yes. Maybe not the same timeline, but definitely the same pressures," she replied.

"Well, it appears that we can help each other, if we can get Steve and Aaron talking again. Let me check on that right away. Who knows? Maybe we'll actually get to work together sometime!"

"That could be interesting," Marcelle agreed.

"Okay, Roger, 10-4, over and out!" Barry said with a laugh.

"Geek! Over and out, space cadet," she replied with a sigh.

"Look who's talking!" Barry signed off with a laugh.

*****

Steven was at his desk, having just ended a call to his backers. He'd been able to negotiate a small deadline extension, but nowhere near enough time to finish the project that he could see. He released the belt holding him into his chair (he hated the pants that had Velcro on the seat!) and hooked himself to the tethers he used when he wanted to relax in the office. They allowed him to float in the microgravity while keeping him from bouncing off the walls.

He had just dropped into a light trance when the communicator beeped.

"Answer," he said.

"Barry here," announced his V.P.

"So, what's the call about? Do you have a miracle on hand?" Steven sighed.

"Maybe," came the surprising answer. "Got a minute to talk?"

Steven untethered himself, moved back to his chair, and looked at the screen. Barry did not show signs of joking but did seem a little worried.

"Yes! You said, 'Maybe'?"

"Yep. Just got a call from my ex-wife, Marcelle, over at Habitat Projects. She was calling me to see if you were willing to talk to Aaron. Seems they're having problems of their own and want to talk to us."

"Talk to that son of a sea cook? He couldn't give me the time of day with a clock in front of him! Just what does he think he can offer me? Or vice versa?" Steven fumed.

"Well," Barry said, "it appears that we have a need that he can fill. And he seems to have a need that we can fill. You see, he lost a tug during the mirror placement and we, of course, have one extra. Also, he can provide us with just the kind of mirror we need to light the Ag section."

Steven, about to blow his top, stopped and thought. The last thing he wanted was to do any kind of deal with Aaron. Their argument about the best way to go about constructing a habitat had gotten out of hand those many years ago. From best of friends, they had become rivals, fighting each other in every non-violent way they could think of.

In spite of himself, Steven still had a kernel of respect for Aaron because of Aaron's strength of conviction. While he hated to admit it, Steven wouldn't have had any respect for him if Aaron had given in to him.

"All right, I'll talk to him. But he must come here to finalize the details, or no deal," Steven declared. "Have him call me first at 1630 Universal Time, tomorrow."

"Okay, I'll set it up. Thanks," Barry replied.

At 1630 U.T. the next day, Steven's communicator beeped.

"Steven here," he answered.

Barry said, "I have Aaron on the line."

"Bring him on."

Aaron's face, serious and tight-lipped, appeared on the screen.

"Steven."

"Aaron."

Silence reigned for a moment, then Aaron's face relaxed a bit, "I assume that Barry told you what happened?"

"Yes."

"And he told you about my proposal?"

"Why don't you run it past me again?"

"Okay. While placing the mirrors, Tug Three was irreparably damaged by a small asteroid. We have no backup tugs and the repairs can't be completed before our funding deadline runs out. We need to place the mirrors and start the spin-up or the project is dead."

"And how does that concern me? I still haven't changed my mind about your project."

"I know. But I understand that you need a mirror for your agricultural section. I can provide that for you fairly quickly, in time to keep your deadlines," Aaron replied.

"And how do you know that?"

Aaron looked at him with mild disgust, "I have my sources, just as you have yours. You can't tell me you didn't know about my problems almost as soon as it happened."

Steven smiled thinly, "Maybe not immediately, but pretty quick. Okay, but I have two conditions."

Aaron's face froze for a second, then resignation appeared. "Name them."

"One: You provide the mirror before I lend the tug."

"Alright. I won't pretend to like it, but I can do that. And second?"

"That you apologize for all your previous actions and statements about the feasibility and profitability of my project."

Aaron's face froze, "And you'll do the same for me?"

Steven smiled, but the smile did not reach his eyes, "After the mirror is set up and tested, of course."

"No. The only way I would even consider that is if you do it at the same time."

"No deal, then."

Aaron thought for a while. Just as Steven thought he was going to refuse, Aaron took a deep breath, "If that's the only way, I'll do it."

Steven was so surprised at the capitulation that he allowed his face to show it, "Are you willing to record a statement to that now?"

"Yes."

Steven was stunned, "Why, after all these years?"

"You really don't understand, do you?" Aaron responded. "This issue is bigger than both of us. It really doesn't matter who's right. With what we saw about the consequences of global warming all those years ago happens, both of our habitats will be needed."

Steven considered, "Yes, you're right. And it seems that the warming is not stopping but getting worse, even with the progress we've made in carbon sequestration. Okay. How soon can you get the mirror to me?"

"If I send one of my tugs, it will take six days." He thought for a moment. "If I attach an automated booster, we can have it to you in half that time. How about this? I'll do the auto-booster and the moment you have it on your radar and verified the trajectory, you send off the tug."

"Fine. And I'll program the tug to auto-boost to you. You'll have the tug within four days," Steven replied.

*****

Two days later, the news media was startled by one of the biggest stories of the year, if not the decade. A joint announcement from Aaron Hawking of Habitat Projects and Steven Samael of Space Solutions had been sent to all the major media outlets. In it, Mr. Hawking announced that he had created a working relationship with Space Solutions, and most surprisingly, apologized for all the disparaging and insulting remarks he had made over the years.

"This is a new era in habitat construction. There is more than enough space for us to coexist," he said. A slight smile left the media in doubt whether the pun was intended.

Even more surprising was a similar statement made one week later by Steven Samael, with Aaron standing at his side. "We have constructed a working agreement that allows us each plenty of room to operate without fear of infringing on each other's space," he said, leaving no doubt that the pun was intended. "We have also reached an agreement in principle to set up a combined research and development team to both create an asteroid mining company and to research a truly effective star drive that allows us to reach other solar systems within the lifetime of humans now living."

*****

Days later, the two men met privately.

"I'm really glad you took the first step. I didn't realize how much I've missed working with you," Steven said.

"Thanks. It wasn't easy but I think we both agree the result will be worth it. And now we've made sure it won't happen again."

They smiled at each other.

Flammifer

Phlome s'Ph'lok stared at the unlit candle on the table and summoned images of fire, then 'pushed' them at the candle. At first, nothing happened, then, gradually, he began to feel warm and suddenly the wick of the candle blazed into flame so fierce that half the candle was gone before he could stop his concentration. Then the flame steadied to a normal size.

Phlome laughed. Ever since he'd been born, fire had a continuing fascination for him. During his birth, the house caught fire. His father had saved his wife, Whrynde, and new born son Phlome, but on the way out, a flaming beam fell and caught him on the calf of his left leg, burning it, and breaking it at the same time. Luckily, the healer, St'ven, had just arrived, along with Master Bard Jorg s'Hari, and they saved all three. Since St'ven had to tend to Whrynde and Phlome first, Ph'lok's leg took lasting hurt, even though the Master Bard knew some healing.

Phlome noticed that he'd felt a bit feverish for a second, just as the candle caught. He'd wondered if he some kind of connection to fire. But it wasn't until his sixteenth birthday that he felt he could control flames. That's what he'd been working on but he didn't want his father to know. Ph'lok had warned him many times that fire was a good servant, but a terrible master.

His mother, Whrynde, came into the room just then to kiss him goodnight and blow out the candle. As a child, Phlome needed a candle kept lit, but he had grown out of that. At the age of twelve, he learned to keep the image of a lit candle in his mind, which comforted him. Now, he didn't even need to think about it; flames appeared as soon as he closed his eyes.

Over the next few days, Phlome kept working with the candle until he could light it without burning most of the candle. Indeed, he got to the point where he could light the candle easily, not having to spend more than a thought to succeed. Then he started small fires in a fire pit he dug about twenty yards in back of the house.

But his younger brother, Phrend, twelve years of age, who had just been moved into a room of his own, was so curious that Phlome had trouble keeping his ability secret.

Later in the week, Phlome went to the Londork market with Whrynde to do some shopping for the upcoming annual Harvest Festival. As she shopped for food and cloth, Phlome looked at jewelry and dresses. When he stopped at one dress stall, his mother looked at him quizzically. Phlome blushed and Whrynde suddenly smiled.

"A present for Ahmenda?"

"Yes. A pretty dress or maybe a bracelet…" he faltered.

"Dresses are tricky if you don't know her size. Jewelry is easier if you're not buying a ring. Necklaces and bracelets work well, or something for the ear. Speaking of clothes, what are you planning to wear?" she asked. "Surely not last festival's outfit!"

"Why not? It still fits."

She looked at him and raised an eyebrow.

"Well, mostly…" he admitted.

"The leggings are fine, but with all the work you've been doing with your father, I can guarantee the shirt and jacket won't fit without major alterations. We'll give those to Phrend; he'll be very happy. How much do you have to spend?"

Ph'lok was a carpenter, and also handy with sculpture and whittling. While Phlome was not as good with the wood sculpting, he turned out to have a fine hand at whittling. And the exercise he got chopping down trees and splitting logs for the home fires had broadened his shoulders and put muscle on his arms.

With his reddish auburn hair, which he had inherited from Whrynde, and hazel eyes, he was accounted a most handsome boy. Ahmenda was a few inches shorter, with a slim figure, light brown hair, and startling blue eyes.

Phlome pulled out his pouch and Whrynde looked into it, then back at him in surprise.

He shrugged.

"I've been saving a bit from each job."

"And doing some on the side?" she asked.

"With Dad's approval!"

She smiled at him, "I'm sure of that. Well, you clearly have enough here to purchase everything you need for yourself, and still be able to buy something very nice for Ahmenda."

"Oh, good! I wasn't sure about that. Can you help me find something at the jewelers?"

"Of course. But let's get your new shirt and a vest rather than a jacket. Less material means less expense."

Phlome smiled. His mother could always be counted on to save pennies without being miserly about her purchases. She quickly located a tailor, and they selected a tan shirt with green piping on the shoulders, arms, and neck, then added a dark brown vest with contrasting white threads on all the seams. Whrynde had him try them on and smiled.

"A very nice choice, if I don't say so myself," Gherre, the tailor, judged.

Whrynde lifted her eyebrows as she looked at him.

"But of course, you do. I've rarely heard a tailor say something doesn't look good on a client unless it's really outrageous!"

Gherre laughed.

"A little bigger than you need, but it will still look good next festival…if you grow a bit more," she said to Phlome.

He paid the tailor and they moved on. At the second jeweler's stall, a necklace caught Phlome's eye.

"Mother? How about this for Ahmenda?"

She looked at the necklace, a simple silver chain with tiger-eye and turquoise beads alternating.

"Very nice! The turquoise matches her eyes. How much?" she asked, turning to the silversmith.

As they haggled, then completed the sale, Phlome looked around the market. Just as he saw Ahmenda, his eye was caught by a striking girl just beyond her. Pale blonde hair, a figure a bit slimmer than Ahmenda, but well-muscled, and a flash of green eyes. But she clung to the arm of a man obviously a blacksmith, so he turned his attention back to Ahmenda. Too late! Her hands were on her hips, she was glaring, and her foot was tapping on the ground.

Whrynde nudged him.

"The necklace! Better now than later."

As he moved, Phlome realized she was right. It would probably put him in better graces if he gave it to her now. He walked up to her.

"So! Looking at other girls?" she greeted him with a scowl and a flip of her hair.

"Not really. I was looking for you, and my attention was caught by her hair," he replied uncomfortably.

She cooled a bit.

"Have you ever seen anyone in Varna with hair like that?" he pointed out. It was a good point. All the women in Varna had either black or brown hair, with the occasional redhead like his mother.

"And besides," he continued, "if I was interested in anyone else why would I have spent my hard-earned coin on this?"

He held out the box to her.

She cooled visibly as she took the box, and when she opened it and saw the necklace, she gasped. She pulled it out slowly, eyes shining, then looked at him with an expression he'd never seen before. Clutching the necklace tightly in one hand, she grabbed him with the other and pulled his head down for a kiss.

Moments later, when the clinch broke, it took him quite a while to recover. Not only had she never given him more than a peck on the cheek, he'd never imagined a kiss like that. He couldn't even think of a way to describe it!

She looked at him, eyes still shining, and then dropped them to the necklace still shining in her other hand.

"It's beautiful!"

"I had meant to give it to you for festival, but now I guess you'll have a chance to find a dress to match."

She gave him a look that made him blush, and the crowd that had gathered around them laughed. As he looked at them, he saw not only his mother, but also the woman and her blacksmith friend who had unintentionally precipitated the incident.

Ahmenda took his arm and they went to Whrynde.

"Hello, Ahmenda. So, do you like your present?" she asked, smiling.

"I love it! Now how am I going to find a dress worthy of it?" she replied.

"Try Seamstress Fahlan. She had some very pretty dresses and gowns, and if none of them match, just show her the necklace. I'm sure she can find or make something appropriate," Whrynde pointed out the stall and Ahmenda, after giving Phlome another, more decorous kiss, walked quickly over.

"That went well. I gather she's never kissed you like that," Whrynde said.

"Kissed me? I never in my life…" Phlome was at a loss for words and blushed again.

"Don't worry, son," she replied. "I knew it was a matter of time before something like that happened. She's a good match for you and you obviously like her."

"Like doesn't even come close after that!" he blushed again. "Maybe I should thank that couple. I don't think something like that could have happened otherwise!"

"You're welcome!" said a pair of voices behind him.

He spun around, surprised to see the couple in question standing behind him.

"My name is Garak s'Golan, and this is Fhome d'Felen, my betrothed. We came here from Durlanta, so I could see what to bring to festival. We couldn't help but notice what happened. That was a beautiful bit of work you gave the young lady. Your betrothed?" the man asked.

Phlome managed not to blush again, but just barely.

"No. I'm interested, and she likes me, but we haven't spoken yet."

"Well, if I know anything about women, she won't say no if you ask," Fhome said to him smiling. "Kisses like that are not bestowed on 'just friends.'"

This time he couldn't help it, he blushed again.

"Don't make this any harder for him," Whrynde interjected. "He's not much older than you, unless I miss my guess."

Now it was Fhome's turn to blush. Phlome couldn't help but notice how good it looked on her.

"I'm sorry," she apologized, looking at him.

"Forgiven," he said with a small bow.

Garak frowned, then looked at them.

"Do you know Ph'lok the carpenter and sculptor?" he asked.

"My husband," Whrynde replied proudly.

"Ah. I've seen some of his work, and it's quite good," Garak said enthusiastically.

"Why, thank you! And you are?"

Unnoticed, Ph'lok had come up to the small group. Phlome made the introductions.

"Oh, now I can see why my son got into some trouble on your account."

Fhome was confused, "I don't! I'm nothing special!"

"My dear, look around. Are there any other women with your hair color in this town?" Garak replied.

Fhome looked around and saw nothing but dark-haired women.

"Oh! Maybe I should have worn something over it…"

"Nonsense! Be proud of your hair, it makes you who you are. At least in part," said Whrynde. "My color is not usual in this village either, but you won't catch me hiding it!"

Ph'lok hugged her with one arm, "No indeed, I wouldn't let her. And you can see that Phlome also has it." This was true. Phlome's hair however was a few shades lighter than his mother's, almost a true red.

Fhome smiled, "You're right. Thank you!"

Garak turned to Ph'lok and said, "I've admired your work in wood. Perhaps we can do something together? I've a few ideas in mind."

The talk turned to shop for the men, so the women wandered off together to shop.

As the days passed, Phlome continued to work on his control, spending at least an hour every evening at the fire pit with larger and larger fires. He also found that he could "sculpt" flames, making them assume rough shapes. And as time went on, Phlome found that he could concentrate the flames into a smaller area, which had the effect of concentrating the heat.

The weekend before festival, he and Phrend took an overnight camping trip. After supper, Phlome showed his brother some of the simpler abilities he was working on. Suddenly, a doe and her fawn ran past, startling him.

Phlome lost control for a moment, and the flames flared out with great intensity, almost catching him and Phrend. He concentrated, brought the flames back to the logs and stopped. He turned to Phrend.

"I think that's enough for now."

He felt a bit of a headache, and a wave of sleepiness. After a few moments, he fell deeply asleep.

Days later, with the rising of the harvest moon, the Festival started. Normally, the guest of honor lit the bonfire. However, this festival's guest, Master Bard Jorg s'Hari, had made an unusual request. Even though he had not been in the area for ten years, the elders reluctantly granted it. After all, none refused the Master Bard!

Phrend had approached the Master Bard on his arrival and explained about Phlome and his talent. He swore the Master Bard to secrecy, and then invited him to watch Phlome at his practice from a secret spot. Phlome had no idea they were there and Jorg was astounded but managed to keep himself and his excitement hidden.

So, at the lighting of the festival bonfire, the Master Bard approached the bonfire with torch in hand. But instead of lighting the fire, he turned to the expectant crowd.

"I am honored more than I can say," he started and was greeting by laughing from the crowd.

"Well, maybe not that much," he said grinning. "But I am going to hand the lighting of the bonfire to a young man with an extraordinary talent. He will do the lighting in a way none of us have ever seen before. Phlome s'Ph'lok, join me, please!"

The crowd gasped and buzzed. The Master Bard giving up the ceremonial lighting to a village boy? Unheard of!

Phlome was equally astounded. He couldn't bring himself to move.

"What is this?" his parents said in unison.

"Just watch," Phrend told them. "You've never seen anything like it!"

He nudged Phlome forward, then when his brother didn't move, took his hand and pulled him out of the crowd to join the Master Bard.

"Sorry to pull this on you, but I really believe that you have an incredible talent that needs to be seen. Don't worry; I'll handle anything people say. Please?" the Master Bard pleaded.

Phlome could not refuse, not since he was already standing in front of the whole crowd. He took the torch from the Master Bard. But instead of thrusting it in the fire, he first damped the flames almost to extinction, and then made them flare brightly. Then he tried something he had only attempted once before. He held out his hand and willed the flames to dance on his bare flesh with no harm.

Phlome blew at the flames on his hand and they flowed the ten feet to the bonfire. They seemed to disappear into the center of the wood, but then the bonfire blazed into life. Gasps of awe greeting this display.

"I give you Phlome s'Ph'lok, Master of Fire!" the Master Bard cried out. "Let him be known as Flammifer!"

He took Phlome's hand and seated him next to his own place of honor. For the next hour, many of his friends and fellow villagers came to express their amazement at seeing this odd, but amazing ability of his. The only thing that truly penetrated his fog of bemusement was the fact that he had not seen Ahmenda yet.

One other odd thing penetrated while he was sitting there, being acknowledged by people. Garak and Fhome came to greet him and express their own amazement. It hardly registered that Fhome was asking many questions about how he had developed and cultivated his ability, but what did register was when she took his hand and kissed him on the cheek. He felt a coolness that came in waves, as if he'd taken a step into the lake on a windy day.

As she walked away, Ahmenda came into view. In a dress of some smooth shiny material in shades of blue and green, with a low-cut neck and a long overskirt with slits showing both the dress beneath and some glimpses of leg. He lost all desire to look at Fhome.

Ahmenda came up to him and kissed him decorously on the cheek, although he at first attempted to capture her lips. Then she sat down next to him and began to ask many of the same questions others had. As he answered them, most of his mind dwelt on her and the way he wished she might treat him.

Suddenly, Phrend came to his other side, shook him, and motioned toward the bonfire. The flames had started to show shapes that mirrored the fantasies he had been dwelling on, and many of the villagers, particularly his parents, were starting to notice.

Startled, he went to quench the flames, but in his haste and excitement, ended up causing a huge flare-up, almost an explosion. He shielded Ahmenda as a cry of pain sounded, then took a deep breath, concentrated, and reduced the flames to their normal size. Then he let all control ease.

As he looked around, he saw that some small fires had started in other places. As the logs had flared up, they spat out sparks and pieces of burning wood.

Concentrating, Phlome put out all the fires he could see. But as he finished, he once again heard cries of pain and realized that they came not from Ahmenda, but from his brother, Phrend!

The Master Bard was tending him, but Phrend had taken a burning ember to his face. Healer St'ven came up and examined him.

"Nothing serious, but he may carry a scar from that," he said. St'ven pulled a small vial out of his pack, smeared a salve on the burned slash that went from below Phrend's left eye near his nose and down his left cheek. "Luckily, the cinder did not touch the eye itself."

"It's my fault," Phlome said bitterly. He turned to Ahmenda, reaching out to her, but she backed away. A cold wind seemed to rush through Phlome's heart as he looked in her eyes and saw concern warring with fear. The fear slowly won out and she continued to back away, slowly shaking her head.

Ahmenda turned away and ran to her parents, her speed picking up until she ran into her mother's arms. Other people were also backing up and turning away, but most were looking at him with pity in their eyes, almost as hard to bear as the fear had been.

He turned back to Phrend and the Master Bard, barely noticing that his parents had joined them.

"I'll never use my power again!" he said, fear and sorrow warring in his heart.

"Don't say that," the Master Bard urged. "I know it seems now that it's all your fault, but I assure you this could have happened, even without you. Why I've seen worse injuries from careless placement of a green log in a bonfire! I remember…" his voice trailed off as he saw Healer St'ven shake his head.

"Well, just don't make any rash decisions," he continued.

"If anything, it's my fault!" Phrend's voice rose clearly above the sound of other voices trying to comfort Phlome.

"How do you figure that?" Phlome asked.

"If I had not shown Master Bard what you could do, and convinced him to have you light the bonfire, this never would have happened!" Phrend asserted vehemently.

"But even if you didn't have this ability, it might have happened anyway, in some unknown fashion," the Master Bard interrupted. "No one is wise enough to know why things happen when and how they do. But to deny a talent only leads to despair, and that is a very dark path to travel."

The expression on the Master Bard's face seemed to indicate a personal experience with that.

"But how can I keep going, learning to control this power? I don't want to hurt anyone else, while I get better at this!"

"Come with us!"

Phlome turned as Garak's voice rang out clearly.

"I have had much experience with fire, both its good and bad uses. I know how to guard against accidents and may even be able to suggest other uses you may not have thought of. For instance, how hot can you make a fire?"

Phlome frowned as he considered the question.

"I don't know. I've rarely tried to make it hotter, mostly I try to control its extent," his voice trailed off. "Can you really help me with this?" he asked Garak hopefully.

"Well, I can't say for sure. As I said, I know what precautions to take, and I have some other ideas of things to try. If you're willing, I could even take you as apprentice. It seems a natural trade for you!" Garak turned to Ph'lok and Whrynde who were standing there, listening.

The Master Bard said, "I think it's got a good idea. It solves many problems," he gestured to the people standing around. "Staying in the village now might not be the best thing."

"Yes," Ph'lok agreed, "but let's talk about this in a more private setting."

He invited them all to their small cottage. Inside, with the door shut, he turned to Phlome and said, "Why did you never tell me about this, son? I thought I raised you better than that!"

"But after time of my birth, you've always been a bit afraid of fire!"

"Not exactly afraid, just very cautious."

"Me, too!" Phlome replied. "I just wanted to wait to tell you until I had more control."

"Let's not worry about that now," Jorg said. "We need to deal with the situation as it is. I agree with Garak that working as his apprentice is a good solution. The only problem is the timing. He cannot afford to leave immediately as his livelihood depends on his business here."

Garak said thoughtfully, "Perhaps we can take care of both problems by having Phlome take apprenticeship now.

He can stay in back of the stall with the small forge, remaining out of sight, and we can spread the story that he ran away."

"No! I have never run away from anything!" Phlome said.

"That's true," Whrynde said, "but we could say that you've left to go visit cousins further inland. No one will think to follow or question that."

"Good idea," St'ven said. "Even better, tell everyone he went on a trip to gather herbs and other medicines for me. He's done that before, and some will be glad he's gone. Meanwhile, he'll be at Garak's tent in hiding, and no one will have reason to look for him or expect that he might be there."

Everyone agreed with that.

"Good. Now how can I get to your tent unseen?"

"Just wait until an hour after moonset!" Phrend said. "Even after all this, while people will still party late, but no one will stay up past then. Wear dark clothes and a black cloak and none will see you!"

Master Bard Jorg smiled at him.

"There speaks the voice of experience!"

Phrend ducked his head and muttered something under his breath as his parents looked at him.

Later that night, after packing a small duffel and sleeping bag as he had for many a camping trip, Phlome put on the dark cloak and made it to Garak's tent without being seen.

Surprisingly, not only was Garak waiting for him, but Fhome was there, too. Garak showed him where to bunk and wished him a good night. He reached out to Fhome, but she said, "I'd just like to ask him a few questions. I'll be right there."

He gave her a hard look but saw something that reassured him.

"No more than a half candle mark, mind you!" Garak cautioned.

She smiled and kissed him.

Much to Phlome's surprise, she then proceeded to ask him questions about his ability, how he had found it, developed it, and learned to control it to the limited extent he had. It was difficult to find ways to explain much of it, but they finished within the specified half candle mark. She left him with sincere thanks.

The next few days followed a pattern. Wake, eat, assist Garak with minor forging, lunch, more work, supper, then trying new things with his ability. He found that he could indeed make normal fires hotter. On the third day, their last at Festival, Garak asked him if he could heat metal without using flame.

"I've never even thought of that!" he replied, astounded. "I can try but can't promise anything."

Garak started him on metals that melted easily. At first, Phlome had little success. Then, on the third try, he closed his eyes and suddenly seemed to see the metal as a bunch of tiny balls. As he concentrated on heating the metal, the\ balls began to bounce against each other, faster and faster. He opened his eyes again and saw the metal shining red. He closed his eyes again and made the balls bounce harder and faster.

When Phlome opened his eyes, he saw a puddle of metal, and Garak was smiling, almost clapping his hands with glee.

"We will start using metals that require more heat and see what you can do. But today we start packing and tomorrow we leave. In order to keep you from being recognized, we will mix coal dust into your hair to disguise the color and give you a patch to put over one eye."

But that last night, just after supper, Garak came to him, frowning.

"There is a young lady asking for you. I didn't tell anyone you're here and tried to claim I don't know you. But she says she was told you were here and will create a disturbance if you don't see her."

"Is it Ahmenda?"

"Yes, I think so, but she is wearing a hooded cloak, so I can't be sure."

"No one else would ask to see me and make such threats. Show her in," Phlome almost smiled.

When she walked in and pushed back the hood, Phlome saw that it was Ahmenda. But she was almost unrecognizable. Her eyes were red and bloodshot, and she looked like she hadn't been taking care of herself.

She handed him a box. He took it, knowing what was coming, but dreading it just the same. He opened it and saw the jeweled necklace.

"I'm sorry, I can't keep this. What you can do scares me! If you never learn to control it, and even of you do, what could happen to me if you ever lost your temper? You could kill me with just a thought!"

He opened his mouth to say he would never do such a thing, but the words stuck in his throat. He could never be sure it wouldn't happen. And he knew that even if he promised her it wouldn't, she could never truly trust him.

"Well, goodbye, then," he said awkwardly. "By the way, how did you find me?"

That at least won a small smile.

"Your mother."

He grimaced, "I should have known. Please don't tell anyone else."

"Of course not! I may not be your girlfriend any longer, but I still think of you as a friend, and would never do something like that!"

"Thank you! And I hope one day we can be more than friends once again."

"I hope so, too," she said, but Phlome could see she didn't believe it herself.

Ahmenda turned to go, and he wanted to call after her to say something, anything that would bring her back. But he knew there was nothing he could say, so he just watched her walk away as tears fell from his eyes.

He turned and saw Fhome, looking at him with sadness and tears brimming in her own eyes. Phlome turned away, went back to the forge, and began packing. She clearly wanted to say something, but didn't. She went back to Garak.

They left the next day at dawn.

As they traveled, Phlome kept working on his ability. As the days passed, he was able to melt harder metals, finally working up to iron. Although it took longer, he was finally able to melt a small ingot, although it took almost a full candle mark the first time. With each succeeding day, it took less time until, after five days, he was able to melt an ingot large enough to form a sword blade in less than a quarter candle mark. Not wanting to waste the molten metal, he did forge a blade under Garak's tutelage.

The one other thing that continued was Fhome's visits and questions about his ability. Finally, after the third day, she confided to him that she had a similar ability, but it worked with water for her. After she left, Phlome realized that explained the cool sensation he'd felt the first time she had touched him.

The next day, Garak came to him and held out a chunk of metal that looked like nothing Phlome had ever seen. It was lumpy and looked a little like iron, but with tints of color. As he took it from Garak, he noticed it was heavier than he'd expected.

Phlome set it on the small anvil, closed his eyes, and "looked" at it. The little balls were an odd color and more tightly packed than he'd seen with the other metals. He was unable to make the balls move more than a little bit. And just that effort gave him a headache worse than any he'd felt before. He was unable to do anything else until the next day.

But each day, he'd try again, trying to make sense of the pattern of balls and find a way to loosen them up. After three more days, they finally reached Durlanta, Fhome and Garak's home village on the coast of the Northern Sea. Phlome was used to the large lake near Londork, Lake Ondo, but he'd never seen so much water. One could see the farther shore of Lake Ondo, but there was no hint of a far shore when he looked west across the sea.

Now Fhome's ability made sense to Phlome. He'd grown up where there was not so much water, but large forests. He realized that something similar, but not the same, was involved with Fhome's ability. He wondered idly what talents might develop in other places.

As the weeks went on, Phlome had no more luck with the strange lump of metal. He did find that none here made any issue of his ability, although he also made efforts to keep it hidden. Only with Garak and Fhome did he use it openly.

But each day, Garak became unhappier and even verbally abusive of Phlome, although he was careful to never do anything physical. And he began to threaten to release Phlome from his apprenticeship.

At last, one evening two months later, Fhome came to him agitated.

"He wants to get rid of you tomorrow! He plans to use a potion to put you to sleep and carry you out to the old ruins north-east of here and leave you there with nothing!"

"And what can I do about that? I have nothing anyway, and I won't use my powers against him!"

"Leave now! I know of some other ruins, unknown to any of my village, about three days east south-east of here. There is shelter, and plenty of game animals. Take these tools and the blade you made and leave tonight!"

Phlome looked at her, "Why do you do this for me?"

"We are more alike than anyone I've ever met. I can do no less. I'll tell him you decided to go back to Londork; he'll believe that you went back for Ahmenda."

She looked at him with pleading in her eyes. Was it his imagination, or did he see something else there? No, just his imagination and wishful thinking.

"I will. But what about you? Won't he do something to you?"

She smiled, an almost taunting smile.

"He can't. I am the daughter of the best fisherman in the village, and the elders would never take his word over mine. And there are other things…" her voice trailed off.

Phlome looked at her again, considering.

"Come with me!" he said impulsively.

She turned her head away and said, "I can't. If we left at the same time, he would hunt for us until he was dead, or we were."

From what Phlome had learned of Garak over the months, he knew she was right.

"And take this," she handed him the strange lump of metal. "He will think you are a thief and will chase you back to Londork. By the time he comes back, you will be long gone with no trace."

"Are you sure you won't come with me? Surely this won't be pleasant for you…"

She looked at him again, but this time, he was sure he'd seen something in her eyes he'd only seen once before when he'd presented the necklace to Ahmenda. Impulsively, Phlome put his hand under her chin, tilted her head up, and kissed her on the lips.

They melted under his for a moment, but then she pushed him away.

"I can't, I won't! Maybe some other time, but for now…"

Phlome nodded.

"I will hope. You know where I'll be. Come look for me there when the time is right."

She nodded, turned, and left.

Phlome packed the few belongings, took the sword, and strange lump of metal, a bow and quiver of arrows he'd made for himself. He left soundlessly. He'd keep going for as long as he could, not sleeping until absolutely necessary. At least he'd never have to hide his ability ever again! Eyes on the horizon, he began the long trek.

Ghost out of the Machine

Glenn Sullivan settled into his acceleration couch as Pilot Greenfield of the *Admiral Farragut* announced the countdown.

"Shenta Field initiation in three, two, one, enga…"

Before he could finish, the ship jerked and spun, defeating even the artificial gravity. Glenn's head hit the side of his couch and his vision went gray. He saw images – a faintly familiar face, odd and disturbing colors and even a faint voice, although he couldn't make out the words.

"Second Engineer Sullivan!" the voice of Captain Sherwald cut through his confusion.

"Heh, here," he responded slowly as the visions faded and he came to his senses. "Second Engineer Sullivan reporting."

A newly promoted second engineer *en route* to his first post, Glenn had just come off shift and was in his cabin.

"Mr. Sullivan, Chief and the First have not responded to Communications."

"What happened, sir?" Glenn asked.

"We don't know," came the reply. "Pilot Greenfield says that we were hit by something during transition."

Glenn's blood ran cold at the words until he realized that he was still alive, and the only question was whether they were under Shenta Drive or still in normal space.

"Are we under drive?" he asked, concerned about the answer.

"Pilot reports that the field was established just before whatever happened did. So with no communication from the Chief and First, we need you to check on Engineering."

"Acknowledged," he replied, unbuckling himself from the couch. Standard procedure dictated everyone to be suited, even though no ship had ever reported a malfunction. "I'll check Engineering Section first."

Making his way back to the stern of the ship, Glenn found the hatch to the section was deformed to the point where he would need a powered jack to force it, or a torch to cut it open. But those were both on the other side of the hatch.

He reported this to Captain Sherwald, who replied, "Change to an EVA suit and go see what happened."

"Aye, sir."

Glenn took off his onboard suit and donned his EVA suit for his walk on the hull of the *Farragut*. He carefully checked to make sure his magna-boots were activated and tested them. It wouldn't do to drift off through sheer carelessness!

"Communications check," came Celia's voice. As the communications officer and Glenn's girlfriend, it was doubly reassuring to have her be in such close contact. Celia Stirlan had a warm, husky voice that went well with her 166 centimeters of height, willowy figure, and auburn hair. That voice came through his com unit very clearly, calming him and reminding him why she was so attractive to him. Under normal circumstances, her voice and looks turned him on, but now, the concern he heard had the effect of reducing the stress he felt.

"Communications, you are coming in loud and clear. Are you receiving me?" he responded.

"Roger, loud and clear. Remember to keep contact with the ship's hull, and watch your head, or we'll lose you outside the Shenta Field."

"Believe me, that's the last thing I want to forget! I don't relish finding out what happens when exiting a Shenta Field while under full hyperdrive," Glenn exclaimed. No person who had done that had ever been heard from again. Even Firlan Shenta himself, caught in an unexpectedly collapsing Field, had disappeared without a trace during a closely observed experiment. Since the Field started at five meters from the hull of the ship, there was no real call to worry. Still, that was why engineers tended to be of medium height, like Glenn himself, at 173 centimeters, with a stocky build and black hair.

As he was apparently the only surviving member of the crew with hyperwave mechanics experience, it was his job to look at the situation and effect whatever repairs were necessary and possible.

"I don't know if I can fix whatever damage I find. so keep the circuit open. When I can, I'll tell you what parts I need."

"Acknowledged. Communications circuit will remain open. Captain Sherwald is right here, and Pilot Greenfield is in the circuit. He's keeping an eye on the Shenta Field while you're out there. Good luck!"

She wouldn't have added that last line for just anyone, especially not with the Captain listening.

Glenn finished his suit check, stepped into the airlock, and started the cycle. The inner door slid smoothly shut and the pumps started. Glenn breathed a sigh of relief. He hadn't been sure that the pumps were undamaged. Whatever had struck the ship just at the moment the Shenta Field came into being had not hit the lock he was using.

On a larger ship, the engine room was much further back. On a medium-sized cargo ship like the *Farragut*, It was much closer to the bow. The *Farragut* could carry up to 25 passengers, but on this trip, there had been none. The passenger cabins were in the area that had suffered the most damage, along with Engineering. Since the third engineer had been left at the last port after suffering multiple fractures in a bar fight, they were short-handed in engineering.

The pumps stopped and the outer lock slid open. Watching where he placed his feet, he made sure the boots held, and then started his journey around the damaged area. The first thing he saw was the huge hole in the hull where the small asteroid had expended its considerable kinetic energy. It was a miracle that the life support and communication systems were still active. Glenn was worried that he would need to fix the hyperwave antenna in order for the emergency distress signal to punch through the Shenta Field. And that was assuming the antenna hadn't been destroyed.

The next thing he saw were the bodies of Chief Thorn and First Engineer Haskins. Shrapnel from the hull had hit the Chief, who had managed to get into a suit, but his heating unit had been damaged, resulting in him freezing. The First had suffered from explosive decompression when the asteroid fragment had bounced and holed his suit. Glenn choked and came close to losing his breakfast. Celia spoke up, worry evident in her voice.

"Glenn! What's happening?"

Glenn looked away, took a deep breath, and got his stomach and emotions under control.

"The damage is considerable. The Chief and First were at their posts when we got hit. Ask the Captain if he wants to retain the bodies. The First is a lost cause, but we may be able to revive the Chief."

He explained the condition of both bodies.

Celia said, "Oh—!"

Her voice muffled as she relayed the request, "He says to see about the antenna first. If we can't do something about that…"

"Roger," Glenn replied. The Captain's point was well taken. If he couldn't repair the antenna, there wouldn't be any reason to worry about two bodies. There would be more joining them soon enough. He moved carefully around the hole, keeping his eyes on the edge. When he reached the other side, he looked up for the antenna.

Glenn screamed! He felt as if his eyes were clawing their way out of their sockets. It was like looking into a pulsating kaleidoscope of colors and shapes. The swirling, *outré* blend of color that the Shenta Field produced was somehow *wrong* and utterly revolting. He tried using a calming technique he had learned as a child that had stood him in good stead many times before, but it had little effect. He clapped his hands up to his eyes and hit himself in the faceplate. The gloves blocked out the sight and Glenn looked down at the hull, reassuring himself of solidity in his universe. He'd never heard of anyone looking out at a Shenta Field from the inside and hadn't known what to expect. The sheer strangeness of the experience shook his sense of reality.

"Glenn! Glenn, what's wrong?"

He dimly realized that Celia had been calling his name for a couple of minutes. "Glenn, are you all right?"

"Uh… I'm all right, Celia."

"What happened? I heard you scream," she asked.

"Don't look up if you go EVA out here. Don't *ever* look at anything but the hull. Just keep your eyes on the hull." He shuddered, "I'm going to check the antenna now."

"Captain Sherwald wants you to come back in."

"No! Sorry, sir, but we have to know what needs to be done out here. I'm almost there."

He worked his way back to the antenna complex, careful to keep his eyes down, but sometimes, it wasn't possible. He managed to keep himself from screaming again, but just barely.

The hyperwave antenna, a concave dish antenna, three meters across, with four helical field guides bolted onto it and evenly spaced one meter in from the rim, had been damaged. There was a large hole in the dish and two of the helical field guides had been badly bent. One was almost totally destroyed.

"Sullivan here. The antenna looks pretty bad, but I think we can fix it from the spares."

Captain Sherwald's voice came back, "I'm not sure that can be done. The spares were in the supply locker, quite close to the Chief's station. You'll have to examine it to see what kind of damage it took. Check it out and see what you can find. How are you feeling? Can you finish the job?"

"No choice, sir," he replied. "I'll manage. I must."

"Not good enough," the captain said. "If you have any problems, stop what you're doing and get back in here!"

"Aye, Captain," he responded. "I'll be careful."

Glenn pulled out his tool kit and detached the antenna assembly, then worked his way back to where the supply locker was. With a ship of that size, it took him a good fifteen minutes to get there. When he arrived, his heart sank. The meteor had not hit at that point, but the explosion had sent shrapnel throughout the area. The supply locker door was intact, but badly dented. It was obvious that the impact had damaged the contents. He found a pry bar and used it to lever the locker door open.

The parabolic dishes were intact, but badly bent. Two of the replacement field guides had miraculously escaped damage, but the other two had been crushed.

"Captain? Second Engineer Sullivan reporting." Glenn took refuge from despair in formal language.

"What's the status, Mr. Sullivan?"

"I've found the locker, but the spares have been damaged! I don't know if I can make them work."

"All right, stay calm. Describe the damage," the captain ordered.

Glenn complied, reporting precisely.

"Okay, bring the stuff back in and let's see what we can do," the captain said.

Glenn made a small box from the supply locker door and some scraps of loose metal. He welded them with the laser torch and packed in the spare parts. Then he used some loose wire to bind the antenna and the box into a single package.

"Communications!" he called out.

"Communications here," Celia responded.

"I won't be able to fit this in through the personnel lock. I'll need the lock to Cargo Bay Two opened."

"But Cargo Bay Two is around the other side of the ship and fourteen meters aft of your position! Will you be able to get there all right?"

"I'll have to," he responded grimly. "That's the closest cargo bay with an airlock large enough to fit the antenna dish."

There was a short pause.

"Request relayed and granted."

Glenn smiled. She hadn't told him to be careful, but she wasn't able to keep the worry out of her voice.

He worked his way out of the ruined engine room and began his walk around the hull. It was difficult to keep his eyes only on the hull; the swirling colors kept making him think that there were things moving out there. But that was impossible…

He was almost to the cargo lock when it happened. Glenn had looked at the package trailing him and was just turning back when a patch of color just to his left became a little more organized and normally colored. In the second before he recovered himself, he thought he saw a face and felt a vibration that was almost a sound.

"Help me!"

Had he really heard that? Or was it just an over-active imagination strained to near-overload by the strangeness of exposure to a naked Shenta Field?

"Communications!"

"Communications here."

It felt good to hear Celia's voice again, and the sound restored his calm.

"Open Cargo Bay Two, please."

"Cargo Bay Two opening," she replied.

Glenn wrestled the package around and loaded it onto the automatic forks extending from the cargo lock. He stepped on them himself and activated the entrance procedure. But just as the lock closed, did he hear the almost-voice again?

"Help me!"

Back in the machine room of the ship, Glenn stepped back from the workbench, shutting off the laser-welding torch as he did. Cutting a patch for the dish had been easy, but now came the hard part of making the reflector smooth and curved to within the proper tolerances. He didn't have a blank mold for the antenna dish. It had never been necessary. But as he looked at the dish, he realized that over half of the reflector was completely undamaged and might still retain the proper tolerances. He took his integrating micrometer and began checking.

Finding that slightly more than one half of the reflector was within the crucial range, Glenn began the task of making a blank based on that portion. It took another four hours, but he finally succeeded.

All that remained was to heat the dish in the inductance oven and impact mold it to the blank. This was accomplished by using an artificial gravity generator with a limited field, spinning both the blank and the red-hot dish above it, then suddenly activating the artificial gravity at five gravities. Two seconds later, he turned off the artificial gravity, the blank was removed, and the dish was subjected to cooling jets of air. After it had cooled sufficiently, Glenn checked the tolerances and found them to be within acceptable limits.

Taking a break in the galley, Glenn was joined by Celia who gave him a tight hug, then sat next to him.

"What did it look like out there?" she asked.

His breath caught as he remembered the first glimpse. "It's almost impossible to describe," he said. "Imagine being in a laserium where the color and shape controls are set for the most disturbing combinations possible. Add a complete lack of perspective or, more accurately, a presence of many perspectives, like old Escher paintings."

"But that doesn't sound like enough to cause what sounded like sheer terror I heard in your voice," Celia said, puzzled.

Glenn shrugged, "I did say it was hard to describe." He thought for a minute longer, "I guess it was just so totally alien, totally unlike the way we normally perceive things. And the shock of seeing it for the first time... Well, it's no wonder I thought I heard voices."

Celia looked at him sharply, "You heard voices out there?"

"Not like hearing them spoken. More like a vibration on the edge of hearing that could have been a voice speaking. It was probably just my imagination. You know how vivid that is," he laughed.

Celia relaxed and laughed, too, "You do have an overactive imagination! You're still nervous walking into dark rooms!"

She snuggled close again and chuckled a bit, "But please, be more careful next time you go out. After all, we still have that date at the Colorfalls in the Black Mountains on Carina Eight!"

He mentally breathed a sigh of relief. It was a good thing he had not mentioned that he had thought he'd seen a face out there. The last thing anyone needed was to be concerned about his sanity. Still, he wondered what had happened. It was true that no one had ever had to do what he had just done, but still Glenn wondered what he had actually perceived.

Was it just his imagination or had he really seen something totally strange and unprecedented? He probably wouldn't find out until he had to go out again and install the antenna. Just in case though, Glenn decided he'd stop in to see the medical officer. But for now… Glenn returned his attention to Celia and snuggled back.

Later, as Glenn was on his way back to the machinist shop, he saw Medical Officer Tanya Sholovsky heading down the corridor away from him. Even with fifteen other people in the crew, he couldn't mistake her petite figure and blonde hair. He called out to get her attention.

"Doc! I was planning to see you later, but as long as you're here, do you have some time?"

"Yes, of course. As a matter of fact, I wanted to see you. I'd like you to take a medical scan. After your EVA in hyperspace, I wanted to see what affect it had on your physiology," she replied.

"Sounds good to me," he replied as he followed her to the medical bay. "I have another question, too."

"Okay… Here we are," she said. "Let's get a comparative scan started. Take off your clothes and lay on the scan table. I'll get it warmed up."

Glenn was thankful that the medicos had realized years ago that an examining table that was warmed to body temperature gave truer readings than when a body was shocked by the cold surface of the table. As he leaned back, the hypno-lights came on and, much to his surprise, the swirling lights triggered the memory of the sight out in the Shenta Field so strongly that he sat bolt upright, his heart racing.

"What's wrong?" Tanya called from her console.

"I'll explain after the scan," he said. "For now, can you just turn off the hypno-lights? I'm sure I'll be able to relax without them."

"Are you positive? I really do need you to be as relaxed as possible."

Glenn leaned back, "Monitor my heart rate. When it gets slow enough, start the scan."

He closed his eyes, took a deep, slow breath, and began the deep relaxation routine he had tried to use while out on the hull.

Later, he heard a voice far away, "Glenn?"

"Yes, Doc?"

"We're done now."

"I'll be up in a minute," he answered slowly, dreamily. Slowly, Glenn began to rise out of the trance.

He opened his eyes. Tanya stood looking at him, curiosity written plainly on her face. He grinned, stretched, stood up, and started dressing.

Tanya couldn't restrain herself, "How did you do that?"

"Do what?" Glenn asked innocently.

She looked at him sternly, "You know what I mean. Not even the hypno-lights put people under that thoroughly. How did you do that?"

"It's just a deep relaxation technique I learned from my father. Was I really that deep?"

Tanya shook her head, "I probably could have done minor surgery if you had needed it! Where did your father learn that?"

"I think he got it from my grandfather, who got it from his father. It's been in my family for I don't know how long. Everyone in the family had learned it by their thirteenth birthday. If you want, I can teach it to you; it's quite simple."

"I'd love that!"

"Love what?" came Celia's voice, sounding suspicious.

Tanya spun around, surprised.

"I'm going to teach her my deep relaxation technique," Glenn said. "It seems to be very effective."

"That's putting it mildly!" Tanya exclaimed.

"How come I never heard about it?" Celia asked.

Glenn shrugged, "I guess I just don't think of it as anything exceptional. It's something I do only when I really need it; it never occurred to me that other people don't know how to do it."

"Can you teach me, too?"

"Sure," Glenn said. "I can even teach it to both of you at the same time."

"Great," Celia smiled. "How about right now?"

"Not right now…"

"No, I need…" Glenn and Tanya spoke simultaneously. They stopped and looked at each other.

"I need to look at the scan comparison," Tanya said.

"I'd like to see them, too," Glenn said.

Celia shrugged.

"Let's all take a look at them," she suggested, going to stand next to Glenn. They walked over to the computer terminal.

"Computer, run comparison analysis of med scan just completed and baseline scan, subject Sullivan, Glenn. Display on screen and print a hard copy. Now, Glenn, you said something about the hypno-lights?"

"Oh! When I was out on the hull, I accidentally looked up at the Shenta Field. It was extremely disturbing, and for a moment, the hypno-lights reminded me of that experience."

"Disturbing?" Celia exclaimed. "I don't think I've ever heard you scream! Not even in some of the virtual reality scenarios they pulled on us in academy refresher courses."

"Fear?" Tanya shook her head. "What could make you respond that way?"

"It wasn't exactly fear; it was shock and surprise. What I saw was totally alien. It looked wrong, somehow, as if I was seeing something no human was meant to see. But what does the scan show?"

Tanya looked at the computer screen.

"I don't see anything unusual. Computer, run comparison again, and display discrepancies only."

The screen blanked for a moment. Three readings came up.

"Now that's strange. Adrenaline is understandable under high stress conditions, but glucose and a higher level of neurotransmitters? Computer. Show increased glucose activity localization."

The screen showed an image of Glenn's body. The increased glucose usage showed mainly in the amygdala.

"Did you have any strange experiences besides looking at the Shenta Field?"

"Well, as a matter of fact," he said hesitantly, "that's what I wanted to talk to you about. As I was coming back in, I thought I saw and heard something."

"What!" Tanya and Celia exclaimed.

"You told me that you heard voices," Celia said, "but not that you saw something. You should have reported that immediately! What did you see?"

"I don't know that I *saw* anything. But it did seem as if the colors for a moment formed a face. And I thought I heard someone say, 'Help me!'"

Celia stared, "But you were out on the hull! Aside from the fact that there's a vacuum out there, the Shenta Field totally scrambles all forms of communications not based on the Field's energies."

"I know," Glenn said as he shrugged. "Now you understand why I'm worried and was uncomfortable about saying anything."

"Well, we could run a new psychological test," Tanya suggested. "It would only take an hour."

Glenn face went pale, "You don't really think…"

"No, I don't. But it never hurts to make sure. Also, when we tell Captain Sherwald, it will help to show the results."

"But what about the rest of the work I need to do on the antenna?"

"It can wait an hour more, can't it?"

Glenn let himself be talked into taking the test. He knew it was the right thing to do, but he was afraid of the findings. He didn't want to be put under the doctor's mind machines. He didn't know exactly what they did, but he knew he was disturbed by the idea.

As it turned out, Glenn had nothing to worry about. The machines did passive measurements of the brain's electrical field. He was under a normal amount of stress, considering the strain he'd experienced. Glenn returned to his work, straightening out the field guides and attaching them to the dish. He worked so efficiently that he was done within a few hours.

"Captain," he called on the intercom.

"Yes, Mr. Sullivan?"

"The hyperwave antenna has been repaired. Do you want to check it, or should I just replace it now?"

"No, not now. I'd take a look, but I trust you. Since you've been working almost a full day including your EVA, I'd rather have you rested. It would be better than sending you out tired. Report back after you've slept and eaten."

"Thank you, sir."

Eight hours later, after a rather restless sleep with some disturbing dreams (including disembodied voices and strange distorted faces), Glenn reported to Captain Sherwald.

"I've been talking to Officers Stirlan and Sholovsky. They tell me you had an interesting experience while on EVA?" the captain inquired.

"Yes, I did," Glenn replied. He told his story again, omitting nothing.

The captain frowned, "Normally, I'd never let you go out alone after that kind of experience, but you're the only one who can do the work. But I'm ordering you to report anything unusual immediately!"

"Yes, sir!"

"Do you need any help out there?" the captain asked.

Glenn considered for a moment, "No, but I will need to use Cargo Bay Two again to bring all the equipment out. I'll keep the suit mike open at all times, sir."

"Do that, Mr. Sullivan. Proceed when ready."

Once again, Glenn suited up. After all the checklists had been completed, he went out of Cargo Bay Two with a strange sense of anticipation and concern. What would happen this time?

Glenn got everything out onto the hull and moved into place without problem. It was just as he was finishing the installation that it happened again.

"Help me!"

This time there was no doubt. He had heard *something*!

"Communications! Did you pick up anything on my audio circuit?"

"No, sir, nothing."

"Scan all frequencies, I'm going to assume something is really out here. See if you can find anything. Report this to the Captain immediately!"

"I'm monitoring, Mr. Sullivan. Are you sure about that?"

"No. But I'll finish working before I do anything further about the distractions."

Without gravity, the work was both easier and harder. The weight was less, but mass still had its normal quotient of inertia. But he had trained for this very kind of thing at the Academy, even if he had never expected to use it. Once finished, he double and triple-checked every part of the installation.

Finally finished, Glenn reported in.

Once again, Captain Sherwald asked if Glenn was still going to try anything.

"I think I have to, sir. I might go equally crazy turning back now!"

Glenn steeled himself to look up. No, it hadn't been his imagination. The colors did seem to be forming a face; one that looked strangely familiar!

"Who are you?"

"Who am I?"

"Yes, who are you?"

"I…I am…I am…"

"Who?" Glenn all but shouted.

Captain Sherwald said, in an aside to Pilot Greenfield, "Check the instruments. Can you see any odd readings?"

"Sir, I'm getting nothing on any band except for a strange fluctuation in the Shenta Field," he replied.

"In the Shenta field?" Glenn asked, amazed.

"Shenta!" the voice almost exploded inside his head. "I am…Shenta!"

Against his will, Glenn looked again. It was true – the face bore an amazing resemblance to the holos of Firlan Shenta! As his eyes met its eyes, Glenn felt as if he were being pulled into a tunnel with a force of three gravities, but nothing happened, except that the face disappeared.

"Communications, what just happened? Did you hear anything?"

"Nothing but your voice, sir," Celia replied.

"There was a momentary fluctuation in the Shenta Field, but it just now stopped!" he heard the pilot say.

Glenn shook his head, "Sir, I'm going to come back in. I request a full medical and psychological evaluation afterward."

"Required, Mr. Sullivan! Report to the MedOff immediately after removing your suit," the captain ordered.

Five hours later, after the most grueling set of tests since the Academy entrance exam, Tanya reported her results to the Captain.

"Sir, I have examined Mr. Sullivan completely, and both the medical lab computer and I agree. There is nothing wrong with him, either physically or mentally. The results of this test agree with the last set I took. He is still showing some aftereffects of adrenaline rush, and there still are elevated levels of glucose usage in the amygdala, but we can see no reason why that should give any cause for alarm."

"I see," said Captain Sherwald. "Well, the Antenna functioned well enough to get the emergency call through. Keep him under observation until we are brought to a repair port, then please confirm your findings with the Base Medical Officer and, if necessary, send your test results and data back to Terra HQ for the surgeon-general's consideration. That will be all."

Glenn, exhausted after the ordeal, went back to his quarters to sleep. He was deep under even as his eyes finished closing. He dreamed.

He found himself walking along the banks of his favorite fishing stream as a child. He was playing with a companion whose face he thought he knew. Then he was in the Academy, studying math with a friendly teacher who guided him along the intricacies of matrix calculus. He knew he should recognize him but couldn't remember the name.

Suddenly, he found himself in a room he knew. A room that only existed as a visualization of his mind, the room of total relaxation. But someone else was with him. He turned to look and saw, "Firlan Shenta?"

The now-familiar looking stranger slowly nodded. "Yes, that was...is...my name. But who are you?"

"Glenn Sullivan, Second Engineer, Terran Space Service, 347-04-9943-03-9951. I studied at Shenta Institute, degreed in advanced hyperwave mechanics."

"Then my theory was correct! The Field translates matter into hyperspace!"

"Yes. That is the basis of the Shenta Drive. But how can you be here?"

"Where is here?" Shenta asked.

"This room only exists in my imagination! It has no basis in reality," Glenn was incredulous.

"Then, by the principle of Occam's Razor, I must be in your imagination and also without basis in reality."

"Then I'm going insane!" Glenn's head pounded with the effort to understand.

"But didn't the medical computers tell you that you are sane?" Shenta asked, reasonably.

"Yes, but how did you know that?" Glenn's temper flared. "If you're only a figment of my imagination, then I can dismiss you!"

He blanked out every thought of Shenta from his mind, and then looked again. Shenta stood there, looking at him calmly.

Glenn fought with the temptation to throw a childish temper tantrum, and as he did, the ridiculousness of the situation struck and he started to laugh. Here he was, arguing with himself! Even arguing with his own imagination!

"Okay, let's say you're real. Then how is it that you are in my mind but not in a physical body?"

Shenta frowned, "That's exactly what I was wondering. The last thing I remember was activating the field for an experiment. After that, I don't remember anything until I felt you."

"Well, that matches up with the stories. They say you accidentally got caught in one of your own fields. You disappeared and there has been no trace of you since. After that, the most stringent precautions have been taken to make sure no one else has ever been caught in a Shenta Field. That's why I was so nervous about going EVA while under Shenta Drive," Glenn explained.

"Why did you do that?"

Glenn explained what had happened to the *Farragut*.

"So, what did I have to lose? Besides, I've never been one to balk at a risk. Anyway, while this is interesting, it doesn't really have any bearing on whether you have some objective reality or not."

"You're right about that. Well, let's see… I think we can assume that somehow this all has to do with the nature of the Shenta Field. Now the Field Equation is…" Shenta frowned, and, as Glenn watched in amazement, a whiteboard appeared and Shenta began to write hyperwave equations on it. Glenn followed them for a while, just watching, then began to be drawn into the work. He had majored in Shenta Field Engineering but had taken an interest in, and minored in, Shenta Field Theory.

"Wait a minute," he said. "That value isn't quite accurate."

He made a notation to one of the equations, "We show that the actual value here is…" and wrote another expression.

Shenta looked at the expression, "Is that a verified value?"

"Yes, it is. It was one of the first modifications of your functions based on observed data. We began to measure…" and the conversation became very technical as two similar minds, trained in the mathematics of Shenta Field theory tried to find an explanation for what happened. The give and take flowed for what seemed like hours, until, finally, they wrote one last expression, then stood back and looked at the results.

Glenn looked at Firlan, "Does this actually say…?"

"Yes, it does. In falling into the Field, I became, to all intents and purposes, a waveform that could only be perceived by someone from inside a Shenta Field. Now, I'm a wave form trapped inside your mind with no independent physical existence."

Glenn looked at Firlan, "Well, since I don't believe in murder and am not certain how I could kill you or kick you out, welcome to my mind."

Glenn stuck out his hand.

Firlan looked at it, shook his head, and laughed. "Thanks! It will be strange, but it's better than the half-life I have been leading."

He took Glenn's hand and shook it. Suddenly, Glenn felt a touch and woke up to find himself looking up into Celia's eyes. He grinned.

"Well, I would have liked to stay asleep a while longer, but as long as you're here."

He pulled her down into his embrace.

Two weeks later, Glenn walked out of the Fomalhaut Medical Center, medical papers in one hand and two tickets to Carina Eight in the other. Celia ran up to meet him.

"Glenn! You're okay?"

He grinned. "Never better," he declared. "I've got a clean bill of health!"

He waved the papers around, "We're ready for Carina Eight, the Colorfalls and you."

As Glenn pulled her in close for a long kiss, he thought he heard a faint wolf-whistling in the back of his mind. She submitted for a moment, and then pushed him back.

"What do you mean, we? Is there something else that happened you're not telling me about?"

"No, just the royal 'we', my dear," he laughed. "There's no one here but me, myself, and I."

As they walked toward the space yacht, Glenn remembered an old, old Earth tune called "Me and My Shadow." He laughed, kissed Celia again, and walked to the waiting ship, whistling the tune as they went.

The Accidental Vampire

Selene looked at herself in the mirror. It had been too long and the thought of paying Norman back would have made her blood boil. She wanted to be sure the effect would be sufficient. The black satin gown fit perfectly. The halter neck showed her shoulders, and the deep V showed just the right amount of cleavage. The thigh high slit exposed her leg well. Now for the makeup.

The deep red lips and nails she had chosen the first time she'd met Norman would make her too recognizable. She wanted him to see her, but not recognize her right away. She took out and applied the pale blue eyeliner and shadow to complement the green of her eyes, then used a green nail polish just a few shades darker.

Finally she arranged her hair to fall across her right eye, *a la* Veronica Lake. Completely unlike the piled mass of platinum blonde hair she had worn the first time they'd met. Looking again in the mirror, she smiled; satisfied that he wouldn't recognize her immediately.

She took a light blue silk shawl that covered her shoulders and cleavage, then went into the late summer night and hailed a cab. She'd been told that Norman would be attending an event at the Ambassador Chicago Hotel, so she gave the cabbie the address. She saw him staring at her in the mirror and smiled to herself, satisfied with the impact her looks had.

Arriving at her destination, Selene followed the signs directing her to the 13th floor for the Computer Professionals Networking Social. Getting off the elevator, she found her way to room 1313, dropping the shawl from her shoulders to her elbows, eliciting outraged and envious glances from other women in the hallway, and distinctly un-outraged stares from their men.

Selene walked into the room and looked around for Norman. As she moved into the room, a hush fell in her vicinity as the men, and even some women stopped talking and stared. A couple of the women even licked their lips, attracted to her in spite of themselves.

Selene hoped she would not have too much trouble recognizing him. He'd been in the background, laughing as she had been taken. The years it took just to find out his name had been wearing, but it didn't show.

Then she saw Norman and started toward him. He didn't quite look the same, but she chalked it up to the fuzziness of memory and continued to move through the crowd.

As Selene approached, men attempted to stop her, but she just brushed past them as if they didn't exist. Her eyes bored into Norman's; he couldn't have looked away even if he'd wanted to.

Norman was not very tall, only about five foot nine, but when she came up to him, they stood eye to eye.

"I'm so glad you showed up," she said.

"You are?"

"Yes. I wasn't sure you'd be here. I've been wanting to talk to you in private."

She took his hand, turned, and started for one of the private rooms that lined two of the walls. She felt an odd thrill at the touch of his hand but attributed it to finding her quarry.

She stepped into the room and closed the door behind him, not noticing the movement in the crowd as she did.

"I've been looking for you for a long time, Norman. You're a difficult man to find."

He said, startled, "But I'm not Nor—"

Before he could finish, Selene had stepped up to him, pulled his head down, and kissed him on the lips. Once again, she felt that thrill, but stronger now. Selene found she was enjoying the kiss. He pulled her closer, clearly enjoying it also, and she felt that odd thrill now at every point of contact.

Telling herself not to get distracted from the mission, Selene's lips moved from his mouth to his neck. She opened her mouth, let her fangs distend, and bit. She sucked and started draining him, and as he passed out, she said, "Payback."

Selene felt him start to go limp. But as he did, she heard the door open and close behind her, and a voice said, "I think you'd better stop now, Selene."

Startled, she did, and turned to see Norman, yes, undeniably him, with that smug grin of his, standing by the door. But then, whom had she just bitten?

"Yes, he really does look like me, doesn't he? We could almost be twins! Good thing I recognized you before you went too far with him. You had me fooled for a moment."

Norman stepped past her and lifted the man onto the bed, then looked closely at the bite marks on his neck.

"Awfully close, Selene. I can't tell if you transferred enough serum to make the full transformation."

"Uh…"

She couldn't quite speak coherently, what with the startlement of the mistake she had made, the rush of lifeblood in her system, and the unfamiliar feeling that still ran through her system from the man's touch and kiss.

"But then who is he?"

"I'm not sure. Let's wake him and find out," Norman replied.

Grant Hughes came to and found himself looking up at a face that was very familiar.

"Feeling better?" it asked.

"I'm not sure. Am I talking to myself?"

For the face he was looking at was almost identical to his own.

"No. I'm Norman Grand. Selene thought you were me. What's your name?" Norman pronounced the name "Sel-uh-nay."

"Grant Hughes."

"Of Hughes Consulting? I've heard interesting things about you. How do you feel?"

Grant sat up slowly.

"I feel very odd. Cold, hungry, but…"

"You've never had so much energy?"

"Yes! I feel like I could run a marathon without stopping, and still have enough energy to make love to three women. Wait. Who is Selene?"

"I am. And I am afraid I've done you a great wrong," came that familiar voice. He looked to his left and was somehow not surprised to see the beautiful blonde.

"What wrong? You kissed me. I've never been kissed by such a beautiful woman. That was wrong?"

"The kiss wasn't wrong. As a matter of fact, I enjoyed it more than I thought I would, especially if you had been Norman. No, it was what I did after I kissed your lips."

The memory of her lips on his throat came back to him vividly. Then he remembered the feeling of the twin stings. He reached up and touched his neck. He could feel the two punctures on his throat.

Grant stared at her, then swiveled his head to look at Norman.

"But there are no such things as vampires!"

Norman looked at him sadly, shaking his head. Grant turned to look at Selene who looked equally sad and more than a little guilty. She smiled at him, and the sight of the pointed canines made him shudder.

"I'm afraid you're wrong," she replied. "We have spent much time and effort to convince humans that we don't exist, and have succeeded to some extent. We do our best to control our cravings and have had success as owners of blood banks and medical clinics. Under certain circumstances, the RNA retrovirus that makes us vampires can affect cures to some diseases that human drugs have no effect on, especially diseases of the blood," Selene told him.

"You mean I'm a vampire now?"

Grant felt ill at the thought.

"We're not sure yet," Selene said. "Norman came into the room looking for me and stopped me before I'd completed the draining. You may yet become a vampire, but you may not. I could complete the process, if you like…"

Selene felt both oddly eager and regretful at the thought.

"I don't want to be made into a vampire! How could I work? What would happen with my friends? I don't want to go around biting people willy-nilly!"

Norman and Selene looked at each other and sighed.

"You may not become a vampire. You may remain fully human, or…" Selene paused mid-sentence.

"Or what?"

Norman turned to him.

"For some people, they become half-vampire. They retain the heightened senses and strength but can continue to eat human food and move about during the day. But the light-sensitivity is still an issue. Ever wonder why some people wear sunglasses all the time?" Norman said.

"You mean—"

"Well, not all of them. But some are," Selene spoke up "So you see, it's not all bad."

Selene could tell Grant still couldn't believe he was having this conversation. She watched him pinch himself really hard.

"I really am sorry, Grant," Selene said to him. She could see from the expression on his face that he was not certain if she were lying. "The good and bad news is that you won't know for three days yet. So by Monday, we should know how you've been affected."

"Oh, great! I have to wait three days? And what do I do for those three days? Am I going to be sleeping during the day and waking all night? Why did you do this to me?"

Selene could see he just kept asking the questions popping into his head; clearly, he couldn't come to grips with the possibility that he might become a vampire.

Selene felt even more abashed and guilty.

"As I said, I thought you were Norman. And since he is the one who made me a vampire…"

"Oh, so that's what you meant when you said, 'payback'? But wait a minute. If he's already a vampire, how could you turn him into one?" Grant put his hand to his head. Selene was pretty sure he didn't have a headache, but she could relate to all the thoughts that must have been swirling in his mind.

"I'm not a vampire," Norman said and he smiled. Grant could see his teeth looked normal, "But I'm afraid Selene was correct in that I caused her to become a vampire. It's a long story, and I don't think it's any of your business."

"Not my business? I may become a vampire because you somehow made Selene one, and her retaliation may have made me one. And you say it's not my business?"

Grant was shaking with anger. Selene reached out and took his hand. He almost snatched it away, but the expression on her face defused most of his anger. And the touch of her hand seemed to arouse other emotions. Keeping her grip, Selene looked at Norman.

"Leave! You and I will settle later."

"Good luck finding me," he replied, sneering.

"I found you this time. Only because Grant was here did you escape my justice! What makes you think I can't find you again?"

The sneer faded as Norman looked into Selene's eyes. Then the color drained from his face, and he backed slowly toward the door. The closer he got, the faster he moved. He disappeared through the door, and as he closed it behind him, they could see him bolt for the main entrance.

Selene turned her attention back to Grant.

"I really am sorry! How can I make it up to you?"

Grant looked into her eyes, clearly attracted to her. She dropped her eyes first.

"Well, I can think of two things right off the top of my head. Maybe something else will come up later."

"And the first is?" she asked.

He took Selene in his arms and kissed her. She didn't quite melt, but definitely kissed him back with a passion that surprised them both.

Sometime later, they broke apart slowly, Grant clearly savoring the feel of both her skin and her dress.

"And the second?"

He laughed happily.

"You will be my date for the rest of the evening. I can't wait to see my friends' expressions with you on my arm!"

Selene laughed also. Had she been able, she would have blushed. But vampires didn't blush.

"It would be my pleasure!"

They left the room, Selene's arm through Grant's, smiling at each other.

New Hope

John put his head down on his desk, closed his eyes, and wished he could pray. Between the problems of getting his research confirmed, and the attempt to get funding to move forward to actual testing, sometimes he just wanted to give up and go somewhere where he was not a well-known figure. He just wanted….

The phone rang. He sighed and picked it up.

"John Ward speaking."

"This is Genevieve Wright from the Office of the President. He would like to meet with you Wednesday to discuss your funding request."

"Who? I don't believe I know you…."

"I'm special assistant to William Fowler, Director of the Office of Science and Technology. If you need, I can have him call you."

"I know him. What's his daughter's name?"

She laughed.

"His son's name is Leslie, but everyone assumes that's a girl's name. He hates it!"

"You got that right!" he laughed. "Okay, that's good enough for me. President Jeffers really wants to meet with me? Has he been briefed on my research?"

"Yes. He's very interested and wants to meet with you, Director Fowler and one or two others."

"Like who?"

"Dr. Andrea Volker and Mr. Walter Jenkins."

"What? But those two…"

She interrupted him.

"They're two of your most outspoken critics. But he wants to see how you handle yourself in the face of determined opposition."

"Hasn't he done his research? I've been in front of quite a few panels of experts who didn't agree with or wouldn't even consider my research."

"Yes, but he needs to see you in person."

"Alright. Wednesday at the White House?"

"No, he wants to meet in your office at Duke University, three o'clock in the afternoon."

"But that will attract all the wrong kind of attention," he said worriedly.

Genevieve laughed again. He liked the sound of her laugh and wondered what she looked like. He guessed he'd find out Wednesday.

"We'll handle that. You just be ready for us."

It was his turn to laugh, and it was a full-bodied one, as the weight that had crushed him mere moments ago seemed to dissolve away.

"I've never been so ready!"

The rest of Monday, all of Tuesday, and Wednesday morning seemed to fly past in spite of all the work that needed to be done. He got the research summaries prepared and arranged to have some appetizers and beverages ready.

At 2:45 p.m. Wednesday, his phone rang.

"Security. We have a party of four calling for you."

"Oh, yes. I was expecting five; you say it's just four?"

"Yes, Dr. Ward."

"Okay. Send them up."

Moments later, there was a knock on his laboratory door. He opened it to see Dr. Andrea Volker, a stocky woman with light brown hair, wide set hazel eyes, a flattened nose, square chin, and thin lips. In her forties, she was not attractive but had a formidable presence. Mr. Walter Jenkins, red hair, green eyes, a straight blade of a nose, thin and pale, about five foot eight. Director Fowler, balding blond hair, ruddy complexion, large nose, and finally a man who bore an amazing resemblance to his father, tall, around fifty, graying brown hair, large forehead, running to fat, but still athletic.

"Come in, all of you! Welcome to my humble abode," he said lightheartedly, "But where's President Jeffers? I thought—"

He was interrupted as the man who looked so much like his father straightened up, took off his coat and hat, and smiled. John gasped in surprise. The non-descript old man transformed in a moment to the President of the United States, Randall Jeffers. He laughed at the expression on John's face.

"Very few people know that in college, I did some work in costume and makeup for a local theater group. And those skills have occasionally stood me in good stead."

John shook his head, amazed, "I'll say! For a moment, I thought my father had come back to life. You must have… Oh, of course, you would have been able to find a picture of him."

"Yes, but managing to look like him, although not enough to cause any undue interest, took a bit of work. Luckily, his coloring was close to mine."

"That's right, you do have similar coloring. But I was hoping to meet Miss Wright. Why didn't she come with you?"

"Covering our tracks. She's with one of my doubles, making a presentation just a few miles away. You'll get to meet her another time."

"Fine, I look forward to it. Meanwhile, would you all like something to nosh on?" he indicated the appetizers. "And if you're thirsty…."

For the next few minutes, they made small talk, snacked, and drank. Finally, John set his drink down and said, "So shall we start?"

President Jeffers smiled, "Yes, let's get to business. I've read your summary, but I'd like you to pretend I haven't, and tell me what you're working on."

"Well, the idea is to collect and amplify zero-point energy, or ZPE, which is found everywhere in the universe. That allows us to not have to carry fuel, which has always been a bugaboo for propulsion systems. Then, the other big issue in accelerating to speeds close to that of light is the issue of increasing mass. According to my research, which follows up on suggestions from the research of Strelnikoff, it may be possible to mediate the action of the Higgs boson to bleed off mass as we accelerate."

"Lastly, using the ZPE, we can theoretically create enough energy to warp space-time locally, creating a frame of reference that allows one to, pardon the expression, surf the currents of space. Essentially, we create a lower density area of space in front of the ship, and a higher area of density behind, which then pushes the ship forward. Since the frame of reference is around the ship, we do not actually move faster than the speed of light…"

"And I say it does and it's not possible to do!" Dr. Volker was vehement. "It does not matter that the so-called 'local frame of reference' is not violating the speed of light. You cannot go faster than light in any frame of reference!"

"Can you prove that?" John asked.

"It was proved by Einstein!"

"Hypothetically, yes. But no one has been able to prove it practically. The argument that we have never found concrete evidence of a particle that goes faster than light does not negate the possibility!" Turning to the President, he said, "I propose to try it. If Dr. Volker is right, my experiment will fail, and nothing will happen. But if I succeed, we will have a true faster-than-light space drive, that could, I say *could*, allow us to reach other stars within the lifetime of most people living today."

Walter Jenkins snorted, "Still sounds like science fiction!"

John smiled, "Don't forget that some of our most common household devices and power sources were once considered science fiction. How about rockets to the moon and Mars, desktop and laptop computers, lasers, and nuclear power?"

Jenkins had to admit that was true.

"All I'm saying," John continued, "is that instead of saying, 'We can't,' I am saying *maybe* we can. All I ask is the funding to make the attempt, even if only with a scale model."

Jeffers frowned, "That's what I think, also. We must at least make an attempt, otherwise we are almost certainly doomed to have most of the human population of the world perish due to any number of catastrophes as a result of global warming; coastal flooding due to rising sea levels, hurricanes and typhoons, not to mention famines from the disruptions of normal growing seasons."

John chimed in, "At least we must make the attempt. None of us want to have it said that we didn't try!"

Even though the expressions on Dr. Volker's and Mr. Jenkins faces showed doubt and skepticism, they slowly nodded their heads.

"So I'd like all of you to be present when Dr. Ward makes his presentation to the House Committee on Appropriations. That will be next Monday, nine o'clock A.M. in the Capitol Building. Will you be there?"

John said immediately, "You can count on me."

Dr. Volker said, "I need to rearrange some appointments, but I will be there."

Walter Jenkins agreed, "Can't say for sure but will make effort to attend. Why Dr. Volker and I to be there, given opposition?"

"To keep the opposition honest. You represent the skeptics, but with the addition of being willing to consider the best interest of the human race. We must keep that present as they try to attack Dr. Ward's ideas." Jeffers looked at them, considering, "If you are not willing to do that, say so now."

Both Dr. Volker and Mr. Jenkins shook their heads.

"We don't hold much hope," Dr. Volker said. "But we are willing to work with Dr. Ward to make sure he has considered all the possibilities, and to make sure he has made no mistakes."

John smiled crookedly, "You mean you want to look more closely at my research and rip it to shreds trying to disprove it. Well, I'm willing to let you do that; it will keep me on my toes and verify my ideas. I'm up for that."

Andrea Volker also smiled, "That may be a little harsh, but maybe you're at least partially right. And if your research holds true, I will do whatever I can to assist you."

Jenkins agreed, although with less enthusiasm.

Ward raised his eyebrows in an expression of mild surprise, then thanked both of them sincerely.

President Jeffers thanked all of them, saying, "I hope everything works out. I plan to ask for funding of a full-scale test but will settle for a half-scale at minimum."

He turned to leave, putting on the coat and hat, seeming to shrink and change as they all walked out the door.

Ward shook his head in amazement, gazing after them.

As the door closed, he picked up his phone, and called his graduate research assistant, David Ford, one of his best friends, and also his mentor, Dr. Jason Redding.

When they arrived, he gave them a summary of the meeting, not mentioning the presence of President Jeffers, but including the presence of Volker and Jenkins, and the meeting at the Capitol.

"Dave, please prepare a PowerPoint presentation, but leave the detailed research to the printed material. I don't want to overwhelm them. Dr. Redding, will you join me at the presentation? Your support will be invaluable."

"Of course. I would be pleased to join you. I haven't seen Dr. Volker in a long time."

Monday came all too soon for John Ward. Still, with the help of Dave and Dr. Redding, he was ready for the presentation. Dr. Volker met him outside the meeting room, but Walter Jenkins was not there.

"No, I haven't heard from him," Dr. Volker said. "I suppose he had an appointment he couldn't reschedule."

"Well, what is, is. Let's go in."

But they were stopped at the door by a guard who first made them all show IDs, then told them to wait. He stepped in through the doors, closing them behind him, while another uniformed guard stood watch. Minutes later, he came out and said, "They're ready for you now."

The three of them filed into the room to face the questioners.

Six hours later, they filed out again, tired and completely unsure of what would happen. All John could think was that they had done their best. Even Dr. Volker seemed worn out. As they stood there, shaken and tired, Ward heard a familiar voice.

"Come on, it wasn't that bad, was it?"

John looked up at Genevieve Wright and felt his breath catch in his throat, his eyes widen, and his jaw drop. She was about five feet seven, slim but not skinny, with honey blonde hair, green eyes, and a straight nose. She was smiling at him, and he felt his tiredness fall away.

He straightened up and smiled back at her. She saw a man about six feet tall, brown hair, hazel eyes, a slightly crooked nose, and strong chin. He was muscular, but not overly so, and had an engaging grin that didn't show in most of the pictures she'd seen.

"Well, it wasn't quite as bad as defending my thesis, but it came uncomfortably close."

"You seemed pretty well prepared, and I think you made a good impression," she said.

He couldn't help raising his eyebrows in surprise.

"A good impression? Were we looking at the same people? I couldn't tell if I made any impression, let alone a good one!"

"I must agree with Dr. Ward," Dr. Volker chimed in. "I've seen my share of committees, but this one…"

She shook her head, "I've seen Sanskrit tablets that were easier to read!"

Genevieve laughed, "I've been around some of those people more times than I care to count. For what it's worth, I think you may get your funding, without having to resort to an executive order."

"I hope you're right!" John said, shaking his head.

"Anyway, I'm here to take all of you to meet with President Jeffers. Please follow me."

With pleasure! John thought, but all he said was, "Lead on."

President Jeffers agreed with Ms. Wright's assessment, but said, "The question now is not if you will get your funding, but when. They report to the House on Thursday, but the funding question could take a couple of months before coming to a vote."

"Months! We need to start the building within a couple of weeks, but days would be better. How can we wait for months?" John shook his head at the vagaries of the political machinations in the U.S. Capitol.

The president smiled again, "The funding from the Congress could take that long. But I've arranged quietly for some alternate sources. You couldn't tell, but there were some cameras allowing a few of the more adventurous venture capitalists and high-tech company representatives to see your presentation. I'm waiting right now to hear…"

The phone rang. Genevieve picked it up.

"Yes? Okay, we were indeed expecting them. Send them in."

Moments later, the door opened, and John was amazed to see Curtis Lang and Cyrus Worthington, two of the most famous venture capitalists on the East Coast. They smiled at him.

"We were impressed with your presentation. How sure are you about your theory?"

"Well, strictly speaking, it's a hypothesis, since there is no experimental-yet. But I'm willing to put up what money I can afford myself, and to invest all my time."

"I also am willing to invest my time into attempting the experiment," Dr. Volker said to John's amazement. "I am willing to work with him to verify his equations and turn them into a test mechanism."

As she was speaking, the phone rang again. Genevieve answered it again and her eyebrows rose as she spoke, "Send them in."

Moments later, the door opened again. In came Aaron Hawkins, followed by April Jones-Hawkins. And trailing behind them, grinning like a fool, was Walter Jenkins with Howard Delacroix, the President of John Ward's own Duke University, and Warren Rockland, President of the Massachusetts Institute of Technology!

John could barely speak, "What? How? I don't…"

Dr. Delacroix smiled, "What Walter failed to mention was that one of his appointments was with me. Originally, I suppose he had a quite different conversation about you in mind, but his conversation with President Jeffers, and Dr. Volker's willingness to consider your claims changed his opinion. He contacted me, and I called Dr. Rockland. We have decided to pool our resources and work with you to get the scale test model built."

"And we can provide the proper facility to work from," Aaron Hawkins said. "We have an asteroid habitat we just finished the raw fashioning on, that would make the ideal building and testing station; large enough, but remote enough to keep any disaster from spreading to the inner system."

April punched him in the arm, and he turned to her, then back to John, and smiled sheepishly, "I didn't really mean that…"

"Yes, you did," John interrupted. "No, it wasn't very tactful of you, but nonetheless, we have no idea what would happen if something did go wrong. I can give you an idea of what we will need, and you can finish outfitting the facility, while Dr. Volker, Mr. Jenkins, and I complete the mathematical check and the engineering specs."

April Jones-Hawkins smiled, "I do apologize for Aaron. He often forgets to put his brain in gear before his mouth, but he means well. I should know; I married him fifteen years ago, in 2035, two years after we finished Habitat One."

"I remember that. Habitat One was one of the reasons I got into physics and engineering. But you must have known it was only a stop-gap measure?"

"Yes, but we didn't want to admit it. Even Steven Samael hoped we could create enough habitats to make a difference. But when he died during the accident constructing Orbital Three, we lost the momentum we needed."

John nodded, saddened, "That is when I started to look for ways to travel to the stars. I still want to make that happen."

"And that's why we want to help you," April replied. "We wanted the same thing, but none of our research ever panned out. Just let us know what you need, and we will do our best to provide it."

John said, "Let's continue this discussion somewhere elsd."

They all agreed and adjourned to John's hotel for in-depth discussions, which turned to technical details of the size of the construction facility and the mechanisms that would be needed once the mathematics were verified and the equipment was designed.

A week later, Prof. Ward, Dr. Volker, and Mr. Jenkins looked at each other across a desk. Ward's expression was one of triumph, Dr. Volker's was one of surprise and pleasure, and Mr. Jenkins was one of chagrin.

"It works! The equations check!" Ward was ecstatic.

"They do," Jenkins replied. "Even though was hoping not, deny them I cannot."

"Yes, they do. And humanity may hope once again," Dr. Volker said.

"But now comes the hard part. We need to design the power plant and the drive mechanisms, and then start the construction. Let's call President Jeffers and see if the additional funding can be approved."

John turned to his computer and placed a call to Genevieve. He had hardly had a chance to talk to her since they started the research. As usual, the sight of her took his breath away. She smiled at him and asked, "So where do we stand?"

"The math works! We can do it!" he almost crowed with pleasure.

"Really? That's fantastic! Let's celebrate…"

John laughed, "All in good time. First we need to meet with President Jeffers about additional funding."

Her face fell, "I'm not sure how to tell you this, but he's not very popular in Congress at the moment. I'm not sure how much he could help."

John also felt his spirits plummet, "Are you saying we can't get an appropriation pushed through?"

"Not exactly. It just may be a bit more difficult than we previously thought."

"Maybe not." Walter spoke up, "Would help if Commonwealth party could influence?"

"Well, it would, if we could get that. Why do you ask?" Genevieve replied.

"Know Faltine's son-in-law. Went to college and on debate team together."

"Can you get a meeting with Mr. Faltine?" John asked.

"Don't know, but will try," he replied.

Two days later, Mr. Jenkins called John at his lab.

"Meet me and Faltine tomorrow?" he asked.

"Well, I had set up a meeting with George Walters for two p.m.," John replied.

"Could join us. If both Walters and Faltine on board, should be able to swing some Congressional support. Would ask?"

"Sure. I'll call you back in a few minutes."

He hung up and called Walters. When he explained what had happened, and made his request, George said, "Of course! I've wanted to meet Mr. Faltine for some time now. We seem to have much in common, I'd like to think we would make a good team and could really make a difference."

Ward called Jenkins back and set up the meeting. The next day, they all met at Walter Jenkins' office in Hagerstown, Maryland. George Walters was reserved and precise in his speech; Jason Faltine was enthusiastic and verbose. In spite of the differences, John could see the two men really did have much in common, and they soon came to an agreement to work with President Jeffers.

John was excited as he called Genevieve later in the afternoon.

"That's fantastic!" she exclaimed. "Are you available this evening? I may be able to arrange a late dinner with President Jeffers."

"Well, I was hoping we could have dinner, just the two of us…"

"I'd love that, too. But let's see if we can do this, and we can go out to a late dessert?"

"Well, okay. Call me back."

The dinner with the President was relaxing, and the news was good. With the work Jeffers had been doing, the additional efforts of Faltine and Walters almost guaranteed that a funding bill would be passed. And the late dessert with Genevieve after President Jeffers left was all he had hoped for; she really liked him! The goodnight kiss would have turned into something else if it hadn't been so late and him under such tight deadlines.

By the next week, their efforts paid off. A funding bill was passed just before the summer recess, and Aaron Hawkins reported that the work on the asteroid base was almost done. John Ward gathered the group that had gotten him to this point; Dr. Volker, Mr. Jenkins, Mr. Faltine, Mr. Walters, David Ford, and Dr. Redding. As Dr. Redding came in, the phone rang, announcing Genevieve Wright.

"Thank you all for coming. On Friday, our team will leave for the asteroid habitat. I'd like to assemble the team that will actually do the work. Dr. Volker and Mr. Ford have already agreed to travel with me. I'd like at least one more person to join us. Mr. Jenkins, Dr. Redding, will you join my team?"

Mr. Jenkins agreed, but Dr. Redding demurred, "I'm too old for that kind of trip. I'm afraid that if I went and stayed too long, my body would change in ways that would keep me from returning."

"How about me?" Genevieve Wright spoke up. "I may not have the technical training needed to do the actual construction, but you still need someone to manage the team and do the administrative work."

John looked at her in surprise. Aside from the good points she made, he realized that neither of them wanted to be so far apart for so long. As he gazed at her considering, the others could see that they were falling in love.

"That sounds like a good idea," Dr. Redding agreed. "Lord knows, once John gets caught up in the design and construction, the day-to-day details tend to slip out of view," he chuckled. Dr. Volker and David agreed that Genevieve would be a valuable addition to the group. John, seeing the handwriting on the wall, and not wanting to be apart from Genny any more time than he had to, agreed.

Friday, they lifted off in the Virgin Galactic orbital shuttle, which took them to the newest habitat, the Von Braun Orbital Ring. From the hub, they took a space tug, an old SLS. booster refitted for orbital and inner system work that brought them to the new facility.

"We ought to have some kind of name for this place, given that we'll be living and working here for the next few months," Genny said.

John agreed, "Do you have any ideas?"

"How about Ward's Folly?"

"Gee, thanks! Maybe 'Spaceward Ho'?" he laughed.

"No, you can't involve me in that bad of a pun," she said.

Dr. Volker spoke up, "How about 'New Hope Station'?"

At first, John couldn't see it. But as he thought about it, the appropriateness of it started to appeal to him, as did the reference to the Star Wars movie.

"I like it. And we can call the ship the New Hope, also."

"Well, let's get it built and tested before we name it anything!" David said.

"Good point! Let's rest for now, then start again at 0900 tomorrow."

After six weeks of dogged, unrelenting work, broken only by the arrival of supplies and technicians, they had a small, computer-operated test ship with the Ward drive installed. Testing was scheduled for the next day. As they relaxed, taking a leisurely dinner, the computer chimed.

John answered the video call and was surprised to see Director Fowler and President Jeffers.

"How are you, sir?" he said, addressing President Jeffers.

"I'm well. We're about to dock. Please arrange to bring us in."

Ward's jaw dropped, "You're here? Docking?"

Jeffers smiled, "I believe I said that."

John swallowed, "Alright. Just the two of you?"

"No, Aaron Hawkins and his wife are with me also."

John turned to Genny, "Can we accommodate them?"

"Yes. Let me make the arrangements."

"No problem," John replied to President Jeffers. "When will you be docking?"

Off camera, Aaron Hawkins voice said, "Thirty minutes, at 1930."

"We'll be ready for you."

When the party entered, John asked, "What brings you to New Hope Station?"

"We heard you were ready to test, and wanted to be present," Director Fowler said. "Since President Jeffers had done so much to facilitate the project, he chose to come along, not without argument, I might add."

Jeffers had the grace to look sheepish, "That's putting it mildly. The Secret Service pitched such a fit, I almost didn't make it onto the shuttle. But since we had the shuttle and its crew vetted and examined thoroughly, they let me go."

John was still amazed, but agreed that it was a good bet, as it was quite unlikely that anyone on the station now, or arriving, was likely to be any kind of agent.

"Alright, we'll show you to your quarters, then let's meet back here and I'll fill you in," he replied.

Once they were all gathered back in the common room, John explained the test plan.

"We launch at 0800 hours, with the ship's route going 90 degrees negative to the ecliptic, in the general direction of the Centauri system…"

Jeffers interrupted, "The Centauri system? What and where is that?"

Aaron spoke up, "The Alpha Centaurus system, sometimes known as the Centauri system, or just Alpha Centauri, is the closest system to our Sun. The ecliptic is a name for the plane in which most of the planets of our solar system orbit the sun. To say 'ninety degrees negative' is another way of saying what most people would call 'down' or 'south' from the ecliptic. That points us in the general direction of Alpha Centauri. It's actually a double star, one of which is slightly larger than Sol, and the other smaller. Still, most astronomers think there is a chance that there may be an earthlike planet there, although we've not been able to find it yet."

"And that will be one of the objectives of the test," John continued. "Since there is no way, at least at present, to communicate with the ship once it's gone superluminal, we will just need to wait for it to come back. Then we can examine the data to see what we've found."

"And how long will that take?"

"Unfortunately," Dr. Volker spoke up, "we don't really know. At best, it will take two weeks, at worst, somewhere around a year. We are hoping for something in the middle, about two months."

"Two months? We can't wait that long!" Jeffers exclaimed.

"We don't really have a choice," Ward replied. "What's the problem?"

Genevieve broke in, "I think I know." She turned to Jeffers, "There's a vote on funding coming up, isn't there?"

"Yes, and we have about five weeks to show some kind of results. Can't we get anything concrete faster than that?"

"I don't think so," John replied. "Remember, even if we could see something as small as the test ship, light from Alpha Centauri takes about four years to reach us. Even if you're elected to a second term, we wouldn't know anything until a year after you get re-elected!"

"So how can we find out anything?"

"The ship is programmed to drop to normal speed at one-week intervals and shoot a laser message to us directly. By timing the intervals, we can estimate the speed with which the ship is proceeding. Of course, only the first and last couple of messages will do any good as the others won't reach us until after the ship returns," John explained.

"I see. So the only thing we can do is wait for two weeks to see or hear something from the ship?" Mr. Wright asked.

"Yes. Nothing else can be done."

"How about a manned mission?" April asked.

Aaron looked at her and said, "There's no difference. And the ship would need to be much bigger to hold life-support equipment, food, water, etc. There's not enough time to build that."

"Well…" John said. "As to that, we've decided to have the New Hope live up to its name. Once the ship was mostly finished, we immediately started on building a set of engines large enough to move this whole facility. We already know it's big enough to accommodate about thirty people with supplies for two years. And everything we could need is already on board."

"Well, almost," Aaron replied with a grin.

"What do you mean?" John asked.

"We read between the lines of your orders and figured out what you were planning." He smiled, "We brought a few things, and a couple of people, you didn't think of."

"Like what?" John asked, heatedly. He was sure he'd thought of everything.

"How about exploration suits? Planning on just opening the airlock and stepping out? And how about weapons to protect from possibly hostile or at least hungry animals? They won't know we're peaceful. So we brought four of the old Z2 exploration suits and made sure they were in shape, then invited a couple of survival experts, one of whom is a Marine, and the other is experienced with many lethal and non-lethal weapons. And we brought some of those, too," Aaron leaned back and smiled.

"George and Lisa Smithers will be arriving in about a month. We figure it will take at least that long before you finish the full-scale drive. And the ship will be available to take back anyone who doesn't want to go…"

John shook his head and smiled ruefully.

"You're right, I didn't think of those things. Glad someone did! And how about you two? Are you coming?"

Aaron smiled at John again.

"I really want to, but April convinced me that we shouldn't; after all, we need to start work on New Hope Two, or whatever we decide to call it. And that will be a much bigger project and facility."

"Bigger? How much bigger?" John asked.

"Oh, about ten times this size…"

"Would hold about two thousand people!" Mr. Volker exclaimed.

Aaron nodded, "If we need to start a colony that would be the minimum size needed. Larger would be better, but not practical in the time allotted. So have you considered how many people and who are to be on the first trip?"

"Oh, yes. As a matter of fact, every time I think about all the things that could go wrong, I think the fewer people who come with me the better. As a matter of fact, I often think only three people are really needed; myself, Dr. Volker, and David."

"Not on your life!"

"No way!"

"You're not leaving me behind?" a chorus of voices rang out.

John was surprised. He had expected Genevieve to speak up, and her voice had rung out a fraction of a second sooner, but the others… Everyone there except President Jeffers had spoken up. And he looked so wistful; John knew he wanted to be on the trip.

"Well, it's a moot point at the moment anyway. We can't really do anything until we've launched the probe and it returns with the information we need," he said. "So everyone get some rest if you want to be at the launch. Remember, 0800 hours Universal Time."

The next morning, everyone was gathered in the control room by 0745.

"Are you going to just start the drive here?" President Jeffers asked curiously.

"No, we have no idea what the actual effects of the field will be, so we're starting her out by using the mass driver," John answered. Seeing the blank look on Jeffers' face, he explained. "It's like a cannon that uses electromagnets to accelerate the probe along a tube. We'll let it get well away from us, about a light minute, before the drive activates."

Jeffers still looked blank, so Dr. Volker took up the explanation while John and David started the launch sequence.

Silence fell as the countdown continued. Moments later, John said, "And we're away!"

"No recoil?" asked Jeffers once more.

"Actually, there was, but so small that we couldn't feel it. Now there's nothing to do but wait while the probe gets to the proper distance before activating the Ward Drive. With a velocity of 350,000 m.p.h., that will take about 31 hours and 50 minutes," John said. "So let's rest and we'll check back tomorrow afternoon."

And the next afternoon, they were all back in the control room watching. Nothing showed in the telescope, and even John looked disappointed. Then he slapped himself in the forehead.

"Of course! It's a light-minute out, so we won't see anything for another minute!"

And at the stated time, the watchers saw a halo of light that changed color from red to blue, then disappeared.

"And now the waiting game begins," John said. "So let's get to work on the full-scale drive."

Since it was impractical to detail someone to watch at all times, John programmed the computer to watch the same area for any sign of return. A general alarm would sound, and another keyed directly to John. With this in place, they were able to devote their full energy to the building and equipping of the New Hope.

The only interruption came when George and Lisa Smithers arrived, along with the exploration suits, and the other supplies that Aaron and April had ordered. The two experts were both rather short, but both were all muscle. They immediately added a training regimen to the work day, so everyone would be in the best physical shape possible by the time of launch.

The only thing that kept it from being a completely happy event was the departure of President Jeffers. He had wanted to stay longer, but the press of business that needed his personal attention, not to mention the two Secret Service agents who were on the flight, demanded his return.

About three weeks later, just after dinner, both alarms went off. They went to the control room and watched as the display showed a reverse of the effect they had seen at launch.

"How do we pick it up?" George asked.

"We don't," John replied. "It's moving too fast, and besides, it will transmit the records of the exploration to us. We can examine them at our leisure."

Since they were close to completion of the construction, it was decided that Genevieve and Dr. Volker would examine the spectroscopy results, photos and videos. So it was three days later that John got an excited call from Dr. Volker. He went to the workroom/lab that had been designated and was surprised to see Dr. Volker looking more excited than he had ever seen her.

"Look at these results!" she almost sang.

Suddenly, it sunk in what he was looking at. In the habitable zone around both stars, there was a planet about 1.2 times the size of Earth, and just enough more massive to have mostly the same composition, but a slightly heavier concentration of metals. And the oxygen level in the atmosphere was about two percent higher than Earth, with about the same amount of CO_2 as Earth before the Industrial Revolution, and a similar amount of water vapor. In short, eminently habitable. And best of all, the orbit indicated the average temperature was about one degree Fahrenheit warmer than Earth and an axial tile of twenty degrees. The climate would average about that of northern Florida and the winters would be less severe.

"That's incredible!" John said. "I knew there was a chance, but to find something like this…"

"The pictures are ready! You have to see this," Ginny called.

They walked over to her station and she said, "Watch this!"

She projected the pictures onto a screen. As the planet rotated, they saw six continents about the size of North America with many large islands, and four large oceans.

None were as big as the Pacific, more the size of the Atlantic Ocean.

The continents were mostly covered with green of various shades; although they could also see some deserts, numerous lakes and rivers, and in the polar regions, white areas indicating snow!

John grabbed Ginny, pulling her out of the chair and whirled her around.

"What a find!" he exulted. He punched an all-speaker call on the intercom and said, "Everyone to the common room. Have we got news!"

By the time they got there, so had everyone else. They displayed and explained the results of the spectroscopic survey, then ran the photos again. By the time the third picture was showing, the whole group was alive with excitement and congratulating John. Aaron ran to the control room and placed a call to President Jeffers. Once they explained the results, he was almost as excited as they were. The reports were downloaded to a panel of eminent scientists for review and confirmation, and the planning started for the first expedition.

"I don't suppose there's any way to take me," Jeffers said, wistfully.

"Not unless you've resigned recently," John joked. But looking at the expression on Jeffers' face, he said, "Maybe not even then. You've got too much to do down there. But I promise, after you've completed your term in office, you'll be the first former president to travel to another planet."

Jeffers' expression lightened, "Well, I guess I'll have to settle for that."

John relented a bit, "Since you can't come with, at least you can come to see us off. Be here on a shuttle in two weeks."

"That soon?"

"Yes, that's when the final preparations will be finished, and we leave," John said.

Two weeks later, the shuttle carrying President Jeffers, Prof. Redding, Mr. Faltine, and Director Walters arrived, along with a representative of the major networks. When John expressed surprise at only one member of the press being there, Ms. Jean Howard smiled and said, "Every one of the networks wanted to send their top reporter, but the shuttle wouldn't hold that many. We were at limit as it is, so they all agreed to let me represent all the networks."

The ceremony was brief, with the last words being spoken by President Jeffers.

"The entire world wishes you luck as you bring new hope in your voyage to this new planet. May you succeed and return safely."

The well-wishers re-boarded the shuttle, which launched and retreated to a safe distance.

In the control room, John rotated New Hope Station, now the Starship New Hope, to the proper orientation. They had already moved to a light-minute out for safety before John started the countdown. The maiden voyage to bring new hope to the world was about to begin. He pressed the launch button.

The Prism of Lost Leng

Sarah Wilmarth hurried to the door of the Derleth House Hotel. The very thought of seeing Harlan again set her heart fluttering and brought a delicious heat to her cheeks. He'd been away for so long, with no word, she had started to despair of ever seeing him again. Even his colleagues had begun to avoid her calls and visits. But at last the message had come, asking her to meet him at the hotel.

She rushed through the revolving door, almost catching her shoulder-length blonde hair, but avoided that with a quick flip of her head. It settled back down against the sky-blue satin blouse tucked into the knee-length, green polished cotton skirt as she slowed to a sedate walk to the registration desk.

"Harlan Willoughby?" she inquired of the desk clerk.

"Room 666," the clerk answered, with an admiring stare.

"Thanks," she replied with a grateful smile, used to such responses to her beauty.

She took the elevator to the sixth floor, turning left as she exited, and knocked on the door, wondering again as she did so why Harlan had chosen such an out of the way hotel when she knew he could afford better. His double professorship in physics and archaeology entitled him to better lodgings, to say nothing of the family house, so near to the grounds of Miskatonic University. After a minute, she knocked again and then finally tried the door, which opened to her touch.

Harlan's tall, lean frame whirled around in the desk chair, his eyes gleaming with anger. On the desk before him was a large, oddly colored crystal prism. She only got a quick glimpse of it before he threw a cloth over it, shoved it into a small table safe, and locked it.

"Why didn't you knock?" he shouted, angrily.

"But I did! And when you didn't answer, I just tried the door!" Sarah said. "I would have thought you'd lock it if you didn't want to be disturbed."

She felt her eyes fill with tears and started to turn away.

"Wait!" she heard Harlan say. She stood facing the door until she felt his hands on her shoulders, turning her to face him. Looking up, his intense blue eyes filled her vision until she couldn't even see his long, aquiline nose or the generous lips. "I'm the one who should be sorry. I was just so wrapped up in my discovery and thought I had locked the door. I'll be more careful next time, but that's no excuse to take it out on you."

His kiss melted her resolve to be stern with him. When the embrace broke, Sara buried her face into his neck,

"But where have you been? What did you discover? It's been more than two years since I've heard from you, and it was a year before that since you left!"

"I'm sorry, darling," Harlan replied. "After I located the clues to find Leng, I got so excited that I left before I knew how long I'd be gone."

"Who is Leng?" she asked.

Harlan chuckled.

"Leng is a where, not a who. It was a fabled city rumored to contain artifacts proving the existence of the Old Ones."

Sarah pushed back from him, looking up at his serious face. It still bore traces of the excitement that she thought had as much to do with her presence as the success of his expedition. Then she noticed with surprise that he was wearing a blue-green turban. She reached up to touch it, but Harlan captured her hand and brought it to his lips for a kiss.

"Oh, not that stuff again!" Sarah's temper flared "I heard way too much talk of lost cities, weird monsters, and outrageous gods from my father and grandfather! Not you, too!"

"But, Sarah! Doesn't it seem to you that with so many references to it in the old tomes, and claims from your father and grandfather, that it might actually exist somewhere? You know the saying, 'Where there's smoke, there's fire?' How could anyone doubt that such places exist somewhere?"

"No! Tell me you haven't read that horrid old Necro-whatever it is!"

Now it was Harlan's turn to step back. The fury on her face made him hold up his hands in a gesture of surrender as she stepped forward. She stopped, her expression of fury slowly melting back to one of concern. She sighed.

"Just promise me you'll never look at that musty old thing again!"

"I promise," he replied. He carefully avoided even the thought of saying that he didn't need to anymore. He now had everything he needed, and the Necronomicon was superfluous.

"Let's go get supper," he continued.

"Around here? Not on your life!" Sarah said.

"No, no, we'll go uptown to someplace better. How about Persian food? We could go to Reza's."

"Yes, that would be delightful! My car is outside, we can take that."

"Okay. By the way, how are the sculptures going? Have you enough pieces for the exhibition you wanted to do?"

Sarah was pleased that he'd asked. She'd been afraid he'd forgotten.

"Almost. You know I've been doing figures from mythology? I started with Roman and Greek styles, like satyrs and fauns and other types of mythical deities and demigods. That went well, and some of the pieces sold almost as soon as I finished them. But about a year ago, I found that the new pieces I started would turn out different than I'd intended."

"Different? How?" Harlan was both startled and curious.

"Oh, I don't really want to talk about that now. Let's just go to dinner."

Driving through the winding streets of Arkham, she finally seemed to calm down. She kept up a stream of inconsequential chatter, telling him about classmates of theirs; who had gotten married, who divorced, who moved away and where to if she knew, and so on.

Harlan listened, asking questions, expressing congratulations and condolences as appropriate and getting back into the flow of civilization. The places he'd been hadn't had access to the usual amenities of life.

Sarah ordered the combination appetizer for them both, then ordered the lamb kabob with dill rice and a glass of dry red wine, while Harlan ordered the combination special of kefta kabob and chicken, also with dill rice. But he ordered the Persian red tea and sweetened it to within an inch of its life.

Even though this was his usual, Sarah wrinkled her nose at him as he kept adding packets of raw sugar. She didn't know how he had developed such a taste but knew she couldn't change that.

"So," she started, "where did you travel? How come you were out of touch for so long?"

Harlan considered what to tell her.

"It took a long time just to figure out a starting point. The first hint came when your grandfather mentioned that the first occurrence of the name 'Leng' came from various traders along the Silk Road. So I first went to the Republic of Azerbaijan in Afghanistan. I wandered the area until I heard rumors of a small tribe that had legends of Leng."

"Afghanistan? Isn't that a dangerous area?"

"Yes, quite! But I was able to disguise myself sufficiently, having mastered the language before I left. The group I sought were on the Russian side of the Caucasus Mountains, well away from the fighting. It took quite a while to gain their trust."

"Oh! So that's why you're wearing a turban?"

Harlan started imperceptibly, then nodded.

"I needed to wear one to blend in," he replied. "I got so used to it, that I hardly even realize that I'm still wearing it.

Anyway, I was able to find that village and obtained more information that took me into remote areas of Tibet, and over the Himalayas into territory disputed as to whether it is in Tibet or China. Luckily, I had learned a fair amount of both languages and was able to make myself understood when asking about Leng. It was there that I found the first living person who knew of Leng, by name C'lag."

C'lag was indeed a person, although Harlan had serious doubts as to his humanity. He suppressed a shudder at the memory of the glimpse he had once gotten past the usual swaddling of robes C'lag had worn. Before Sarah noticed the hesitation, he proceeded.

"I was able to get a map from C'lag, although he wouldn't guide me. But the route to Leng was clear. He even warned me about the Yeti!"

Well, "yeti" was as close as she would be able to understand. He'd had a glimpse of the creature, which had almost caused him to give up the quest then and there. While he was talking, the waiter had brought their food. But when he caught the word "Leng," he blanched and almost dropped Harlan's plate. Harlan looked at him, but the man had turned and hurried away. Harlan frowned to himself. The man had a cast to his features that seemed familiar, but he didn't know why.

"It turns out that 'Leng' is both the name of a city and the name of the plateau on which it is located. The plateau is almost inaccessible. It took weeks of searching before I could find a bridge to cross. But it was so old and dilapidated that I took the precaution of attaching a very long rope to a rock pillar only ten feet away. As I stepped out onto the bridge, it seemed that it would hold at least long enough to reach the other side, about thirty feet away. But I was wrong!"

Sarah was fascinated. She had rarely heard Harlan speak so compellingly.

"What happened?" she asked, begging him with her eyes to continue.

"I got about ten feet out when I heard the creaking. I had just turned around to start back when the ropes unraveled."

"Luckily, I had taken a couple of turns of my rope around my waist and left wrist. So when the bridge broke, I was solidly attached, Still, the fall swung me full force into the rock wall."

Sarah gasped, "Did you break anything?"

Harlan grimaced, "At first, I didn't think so. But when I reached up with my right hand to pull myself back to the ledge, I could feel the pain in my ribs."

He put his hand on the left side, indicating the upper ribs, "I almost blacked out from the pain but it's a good thing I didn't. A fall of more than a thousand feet would have meant the end. Even now, I still feel the twinge of pain sometimes."

She reached across the table, placing a hand on the spot he'd indicated.

"I'm glad you didn't lose your grip, or I'd have lost you."

"Yes. That's what kept me going more than once. I had to get back to you."

He shook himself like a wet dog.

Suddenly, the waiter came back to the table with the manager in tow.

"You must leave," the manager announced.

"But why? We haven't even finished our dinner!" Sarah said, perplexed.

"You have said forbidden word," the waiter announced. The manager nodded agreement and added, "We will give you boxes for the food and cups for the drink."

Harlan looked more closely at the waiter and suddenly recognized the cast of the man's features. Harlan looked at her and said, "Yes, we should leave."

Perplexed, she just looked at him while the food and drink were packed, then they left the restaurant. Harlan guided them to her car and had her drive to a park along the Miskatonic River. It was twilight when they sat on a bench and finished their supper.

"What was that all about?" Sarah asked.

"That waiter was from the area in Afghanistan I told you about. He heard me say, 'Leng.' In their land, it is forbidden to speak of it or even hear it said. If we had stayed, I can't say what other kinds of action he might have taken."

"But why does it matter? It's just a place!"

Again, Harlan had to choose what to tell her.

"They have many superstitions that would seem odd to us. To them, even the mention of the place could bring horrific events that they wouldn't even speak of. In a population of thousands, there was only one person I could speak openly to about Leng, and even then, we had to be in a cave located miles from the town."

Sarah shook her head, "So how did you get back up to the ledge? To say nothing of reaching the plateau."

At that moment, her cell phone rang.

"Uncle Randolph! How are you? What? Yes, he's with me. Now?"

She looked at Harlan and moved the phone away from her mouth, "Uncle Randolph wants to see you. He got word that you had returned and wants to see you tonight. But I was hoping we could spend the evening together."

"I'd like nothing better. But my ribs are not fully healed, and my head…"

"What happened? Are you alright?"

She reached out to touch the turban, but Harlan gently blocked her hand.

"I had a head injury while I was in Leng, and it's not fully healed. The lightest touch brings intense pain. Please don't worry, I have an appointment to have it looked at. But I'd be happy to see your uncle, if it's alright with you."

Sarah looked at him and pouted. She had missed him so much! But she knew she would have more time with him.

"Alright, I'll take you there, but you must tell me how you got to Leng while I drive."

"I will."

"Good. Uncle Randolph? Yes, I'll bring him over. We'll be there in twenty minutes."

As they walked back to Sarah's car, they were both aware of the strange shadows cast by the trees. The rustling of the leaves, the tendrils of fog creeping in and the cries of birds along the shore of the river combined to create an eerie atmosphere. There was even the eerie cry of a loon from somewhere nearby. And the story that Harlan continued to tell contributed to it.

"I slowly and painfully pulled myself up onto the ledge. After resting for a while, I continued to explore the ridge that surrounded the plateau," Harlan said. "The gap varied between twenty to fifty feet. I found no other bridges, and finally, my way was blocked by a sheer ridge of stone that appeared to be insurmountable."

"It connected to the plateau, but the blocks of stone that made the barrier were too huge to be man-made and too slick to climb. Then I remembered the descriptions of the cyclopean basalt blocks described by your great-grandfather's colleagues when they explored the Mountains of Madness. The surfaces were smooth with no projections and the grappling hooks found no purchase no matter how much I tried.

"But I persevered. I finally started to climb along the edge of the rock wall bordering the blocks. And I found it!"

At this point, they reached Sarah's car. As she drove, Harlan continued his story.

"Imagine my amazement when I found a door in the stones! This was an opening of some twenty feet in height. The rock that made the door was broken and crumbled, leaving an opening about ten feet up that I was able to climb through. It led into a tunnel of twelve feet wide running in the direction of the plateau."

"I took out my flashlight and examined the floor and walls. The walls were nothing odd, but the floor! It appeared smooth, but as I followed it, I could feel odd groves running along it, just slim enough that my foot would not fit in. And though it obviously had not been trodden for ages, still I felt a slickness to the surface. It was difficult to keep my footing and twice I almost fell."

"After what I thought was three hours, I came to the end. Another opening like the first showed in the weakening beam of my flashlight, and I passed through it to find myself in the lost city of Leng!" Sarah was so startled she inadvertently swerved to the left, prompting a honk from the SUV coming from behind in the left lane. She straightened out and glanced over at Harlan. She saw excitement, pride, and fear.

"But surely you expected to find it? Especially after finding those huge blocks."

"Yes, but it was so beyond what I expected to find that I couldn't believe my eyes at first."

"And what did it look like?" Sarah found herself intensely curious in spite of her dislike of the subject. But he was so excited that she found herself drawn into the story.

"When I emerged and looked around, my first reaction was amazement. Most of Leng was in ruins, but I could see the outlines of the structures. Some of the buildings, especially the larger ones, were still in decent repair. Naturally, most of these were built of the same cyclopean blocks of stone that formed the tunnel."

"At that point, I had to turn off my flashlight to save the batteries. And then came the first surprise. While night had fallen during the time I traversed the tunnel, I found I could still see."

"But how?" asked Sarah. "There couldn't have been lighting that could survive the thousands of years that must have passed!"

"Tens of thousands of years or more, I'd say. Some of the guesses of their age made by your great-granfather and his colleagues are so large as to be almost inconceivable. No, what I found were two kinds of lighting."

Harlan fell silent for a moment.

"The first kind seemed to be a type of stone that glowed on its own."

"Was it radioactive?" Sarah asked.

"That was my first thought, too, but I had brought a Geiger counter with me, and nothing registered high enough. No, this was a type of stone previously unknown to man. The color was odd, too; a kind of greenish-blue light."

"Like turquoise!"

"No. This was so odd that at first I felt nauseous. But I got used to it eventually. The other lighting was stranger than the stone. An odd, luminous fungal growth lined many of the edges and ceilings of the buildings, so I was even able to see inside some of the structures."

"I entered one of the human-sized structures that seemed to be an antechamber to one of the cyclopean buildings. It was then I learned that the growth was not solidly fixed to the ceilings. As I stepped in, one of the pieces of growth fell from the ceiling, narrowly missing me. It struck the floor with an odd squishing sound. I almost stepped on it but managed to avoid that. And a few moments later, one had landed directly on my head. That's what caused the pain."

"What was it?" Sarah asked, startling him. He hadn't realized he'd been silent for minutes until he saw that they were almost at her uncle's house. Like many of the old houses in Arkham, it was a large structure, slightly run down but still handsome with a gambrel roof.

"I don't know for sure. That's one of the reasons I wanted to talk to your Uncle Randolph. He might be able to tell me."

"That's possible," Sarah said.

The door was opened by the butler Groton, an odd-looking man in a suit that had once been new but now was badly in need of mending. Sarah had never liked him because an odd fishy smell seemed to exude from him at all times.

"Uncle Randolph is expecting us," she told him.

"Indeed, I am! Hello, Sarah dear."

Randolph Carter was tall and thin, with vivid blue eyes, a high brow, and a narrow chin. His silver hair was combed back and he made a striking figure. He gave Sarah a quick hug and turned to Harlan.

"So this is your young man? I hear you have traveled far," Randolph said, reaching out to shake his hand.

"Harlan Willoughby," Sarah introduced them, "my uncle, Randolph Carter."

"I'm not really her uncle, but I've known her for so long, I think of her as my niece and she thinks of me as her uncle. Have you traveled to the east?"

"Indeed. I found the lost city of Leng!"

An expression of startlement crossed the man's face, replaced by one of intense interest.

"You must tell me more! Sarah, will you lead him to the study while I have Groton get refreshments?"

"Surely, Uncle."

As she led Harlan down the hall, he saw a number of paintings on the walls, many of which bore an interesting resemblance to the man he had just met. While they all had the name of Carter, a few of them bore a most remarkable resemblance to him. Most of these had the name "Randolph Carter" on the nameplate.

As they entered the study with its large wooden desk, bookshelves lining most of the walls and one large portrait behind the desk, depicting the famous Captain Randolph Carter in uniform, Sarah's phone sounded. She looked at it and exclaimed, "Oh, bother!"

"What?" Harlan asked.

"I have an appointment with my doctor now. Can I leave you with Uncle Randolph for an hour or so?"

"Now? At seven o'clock at night? What kind of doctor keeps that kind of hours?" Harlan asked in amazement.

"He's kind of a psychiatrist. When I first started having those odd dreams, I asked around and got his name. I've been seeing him for about nine months now."

"And his name?"

"Dr. Hotep," Sarah replied. "Dr. N. L. Hotep."

Harlan experienced an odd sense of recognition, "Is he Egyptian?"

"I'm not sure. But he's very striking in appearance," she replied. "He's very tall, with incredibly dark skin. He doesn't look like an African, but that skin," her voice trailed off. "Anyway, he's been a huge help, and the hours don't interrupt with all the other things I'm doing, so it's not a problem. Don't worry, I'll be back soon enough, and you can talk to Uncle Randolph while I'm gone. I'm sure I'd find it boring anyway."

"Yes, you should go see Dr. Hotep, especially if he's been helping with those dreams," Uncle Randolph's voice came from behind them, startling Sarah. "I have many questions for Harlan, and it would be better if we talked alone while you to go see the doctor."

She agreed, gave him a quick peck on the cheek, then gave a more intimate kiss to Harlan, and departed. They watched her go with expressions that matched their different feelings about her. Harlan's expression was one of love and longing while Randolph's was one of fondness.

Randolph turned and sat behind the desk, motioning Harlan to a seat on the other side, his eyes gleaming with anticipation.

"So what prompted this search?" he asked.

"A dream," Harlan replied.

"Ah! Of course. So many quests start with a dream. Tell me," Randolph said.

"Like many dreams, the memory has faded. But I do remember a tall, dark man talking about the fabled city, and somehow I knew that if I searched, I would find it and receive something of immense value."

"And have you?"

"Well, I did find the city, and I found something there that I was able to bring back with me, although it was difficult to get it into the country."

"I imagine! 'A tall, dark man,' you said?"

"Yes. Skin so dark it almost seemed to drink in all the light around us. That I'll never forget!"

Randolph went pale as Harlan spoke. He swung around in the swivel chair, got up, and went to the bookcase. After a few moments, he pulled out a book and brought it back to the desk. Flipping through the pages, he suddenly stopped and looked at something. He turned the book around and pushed it at Harlan.

Harlan looked and gasped. On the left-hand page was an illustration that looked almost exactly like the man from his dream! And beneath the illustration was the word "Nyarlathotep". Reading the text on the following page, he saw "An illustration of the most humanoid of Nyarlathotep's incarnations. He often appears in dreams, although he has been known to appear in physical form on Earth."

Harlan went as pale as Randolph.

"That's him! How can that be? And there is something familiar about the name…"

"As it says here, he can appear in dreams. And you have seen the name in your researches," Randolph suggested.

"Yes, I'm sure I did. But still," Harlan's voice trailed off.

"Tell me about your travels. You must have seen some amazing things, met strange, and interesting people!"

"Most assuredly! It started like this…" and Harlan told the same story he had related to Sarah, but with some additional details that he had left out. He felt that Randolph needed to know the full story.

As Sarah entered Dr. Hotep's office, she was struck once more by his amazing looks. He was as dark as the darkest black man she'd ever seen, but his features showed no trace of African blood. Instead, he could have passed for any white man.

"And how are you today?" he asked.

"Much better! But I had another odd dream last night. It was so odd and horrifying that once it woke me up, I was unable to get back to sleep."

"Can you tell me what it was about?" he asked curiously, taking out a tablet computer and making notes.

"Not really. I don't remember a theme, just a series of images. I think they were related, but I can't figure out any common thread. I did sketch one of the images and did a new sculpture from it."

Dr. Hotep looked intensely interested, "What kind of images?"

"One was a large grouping of bubbles that were somehow connected and alive. I didn't get a sense of how large the grouping was, but I thought it could be any size the intelligence wanted from the size of a man to the size of a planet! I can't imagine how this could be, but I was sure of it," Sarah shuddered. "Another was a beautiful oriental woman with a fan, but I had the sense that this was just an illusion hiding something truly horrible."

"Very interesting! Anything else?" Dr. Hotep inquired.

"Well," Sarah hesitated.

"Come now. You know you can tell me anything!"

"I thought for a moment I saw a figure that looked like you!"

Dr. Hotep chuckled for a second, then resumed his normal intense expression, "That's not unusual. Most people who are in therapy often see their therapist in dreams. Were any of these the subject of your sculpture?"

"No. That one was very unusual. It was a figure that resembled you, but instead of a face, there was just a long tentacle that seemed to have eyes, nose, and mouth, and the feeling of horror when I saw it was what woke me up. When I couldn't get back to sleep, I went into the studio and sculpted it. I was hoping it would help, but it just made things worse. I was about to destroy it when my boyfriend called me to let me know he'd returned. I went to see him, and he told me something of his travels. We went to supper, then to see my uncle, Randolph Carter."

At this name, Dr. Hotep gave a small start and an involuntary exclamation escaped his lips.

Sarah looked at him curiously.

"Do you know him?" she asked.

"No, but the name is familiar. I think a relative of mine may have known him, as that name is known to me, but it couldn't be him. This was more than sixty years ago."

"Oh! That would have been his grandfather then. There have been many Randolph Carters in the family. He was friends with my grandfather."

"Oh, yes. That would be Albert Wilmarth, yes?"

Sarah was surprised, "Why yes! How did you know?"

"The same way I knew of Randolph Carter. And I did take time to do some research on your family when I took you on as a client. Now I'm very curious about this sculpture of yours. Is there any chance I could see it tonight?"

"Tonight? No, it's quite late and I want to see my boyfriend again. How about tomorrow?"

Dr. Hotep looked disappointed, "I suppose that could work. About the same time tomorrow? We could meet at your studio."

"I suppose. Yes, that would be fine."

Sarah left, vague feelings of foreboding running through her mind. They persisted as she drove back to Uncle Randolph's house. When she arrived, Groton opened the door, then indicated she should go to the study. She entered to find Harlan and her uncle looking at something on the desk with their backs to her. She heard the words "Mi-Go" and a gasp of surprise escaped her. Both men turned around. Harlan came up to her and gave her a big hug and kiss. She returned it happily.

"What were you talking about? Did I hear you say 'Mi-Go'?"

"Yes, why?" Harlan asked.

"Oh, that was what I named one of my more *outré* sculptures."

"Really?" Uncle Randolph's voice evinced surprise. "Why did you do that?"

"It was the name I heard it called in my dream. It was very vaguely humanoid, but only because it was upright and stood on two, I suppose you could call them legs."

Another exclamation of surprise, this time from both men. They turned to the book, and flipped pages. They kept turning pages until they reached one that had an illustration on it. They stepped back so she could look. She didn't quite faint, but Sarah felt a shock and put a hand on the desk. There was the exact image from her dream! She looked closer, trembling. No, not exact, but so close she knew it was the same kind of being, like the difference between one human and another.

"Yes, that's it!" she said in a voice that trembled.

The two men looked at each other.

"I think," Harlan said, "that we need to see your sculptures."

"Dr. Hotep wants to see them, too. I told him to come to my studio at seven tomorrow night. Why don't you come then also?"

"A good idea," Uncle Randolph agreed. "I'd be interested to meet him. By the way, do you have his card?"

"Sure! Here you go. I don't know why he uses cards. So many people just give their email address or v-card."

She handed him the card.

His eyes widened, then narrowed as he looked at it, then handed the card to Harlan with no comment. Harlan took it and read, "Dr. N. L. Hotep, Dream therapist, Occult consultant." He raised his eyebrows as he looked at Sarah.

"How did you find him?" he asked.

Surprisingly, it was Randolph who answered.

"When she started having the dreams and it affected her art, she came to me. But it was Groton who found him."

"How did he find the right kind of person? I wouldn't have thought he would know anyone like that."

"I never asked. Groton told me he had helped many of his friends with such issues, and I took him at his word."

"He has been a big help," Sarah asserted. "The dreams don't come as often, and they are not so horrible when they do. Actually, he is the one who recommended I sculpt them."

The two men looked at each other, seeming to come to an understanding without speaking.

"I'm sure we'd like to meet him, too. What time?" Harlan asked.

"Same time as tonight, seven o'clock," Sarah told them.

"We'll be there. But now I think we need to call it a night. I'm worn out from a long day, and I have much to do tomorrow," Harlan said. "But I promise that soon we will spend much more time together."

As they left, the weather seemed to match Sarah's mood. It was a gloomy night with a crescent moon peeking out from behind the clouds and a light rain was falling. Off in the north, they could see lightning streaking across the sky and a dense fog began to creep in.

Sarah dropped Harlan off at the Derleth House, then went back to her studio loft. She had drawn the curtains that separated the living area from the studio and found herself glad of that. Normally, she liked to see her work, even the weird stuff, but tonight she didn't.

Her sleep was disturbed by dreams, none of which she remembered as vividly as usual, but the one that woke her up at six in the morning was very disturbing and somehow involved Harlan. But she couldn't remember what was so disturbing about it.

She got up, showered, got dressed in her working clothes (hardly noticing she was doing so), then ate breakfast. In her mind, she was already planning the new sculpture. *It would just be a bust*, she thought. Maybe from the shoulders up. Finished with her meal, she opened the curtains and assembled her tools. She was so in the zone that she didn't even see what she was creating on a conscious level. She held the image in her mind and let her hands do the work they were so capable of.

Sarah paused for lunch, then went back to her sculpting. She finished up about three thirty and put the finished bust in the kiln for firing, setting the temperature, and timer so it would be ready to show in the evening. Stripping off her work clothes, she went to her closet to choose what to wear for the evening. Since she wasn't sure whether they would be going out for dinner, she passed up the fancy dresses and settled on a simple blue cotton jumpsuit.

The phone rang, and she almost ran to grab it.

"Sarah?" came Randolph Carter's voice.

"Oh, hello, Uncle," she replied.

Hearing the tone of her voice, he chuckled, "Hoping it was Harlan, were you?"

"Well," she started.

"It's alright. I'd have been surprised if you weren't. Anyway, I thought I would bring something to your place for dinner with you and Harlan. Then we don't have to travel back and forth, and Dr. Hotep can just join us for the show."

"Oh! Yes, that would be fine. I'll call Harlan and let him know," Sarah started.

"No, let me call him. I have a few things I wanted to discuss with him. We'll plan to be there at six o'clock. Does that work for you?"

"Oh, yes, that's plenty of time. What are you bringing?" she asked.

Randolph chuckled, "Let it be my surprise. See you at six."

Sarah sighed, "Alright, have your little mystery. I'll expect you then."

"I'll be there," Randolph hung up.

Sarah looked at the clock. It was only four-thirty, so she went to the kiln. It was just shutting off, so she went into the exhibit space and moved things around to maximize the effect of the reveal. Since some of the pieces were heavy, this took another half-hour. She went back to the kiln and putting on a pair of mitts, took it out, put it on a stand, then threw a piece of cloth over the bust. She couldn't have said why she did, it just felt right. She put it where it would be the last piece to reveal.

When the bell rang at six, she opened the door and gasped in surprise. Carrying some bags and grinning at her was her father, Aaron Wilmarth!

"Daddy! You're back!" Sarah gave her father a powerful hug. Luckily, he had managed to set the bags down before she did so, or they would have fallen, damaging whatever was in there. He returned the hug and kissed her cheek. He was a large man, stout rather than fat, with a grizzled beard going gray, green eyes, and graying black hair. He didn't look much like Sarah until one noticed the similarity of the facial features and expressions.

"How are you? How is the *Searcher*?" she asked. The *Searcher* was her father's sailing ship. Contrary to the normal vocations of the family, Aaron was a sailor rather than a scholar, although he did still show some scholarly bent. He seemed more of an incarnation of Captain Randolph Carter than Albert Wilmarth. And his friend Randolph was more like Albert than his namesake.

"Ah, the *Searcher*. She's just fine! Handles the weather and waves like a dancer but misses her favorite sea-sprite. When will you come out again?"

Sarah laughed delightedly. After Harlan and her sculpture, she loved sailing on the *Searcher*. The open seas held a fascination for her that few other things did.

"Soon," she replied. "I miss her, too! But we have other things to take care of first."

She turned to the others, greeting Uncle Randolph with a more demure hug than the one for her father, and gave Harlan a kiss that promised more and a hug that made him wince in pain.

"Oh dear! I'm so sorry, I forgot about your ribs!" she cried, reproaching herself.

Harlan smiled down at her, "A little pain from such a warm hug is more than bearable. Pay no attention to it."

They turned to the kitchen where her father and Uncle Randolph were unpacking the bags. Sarah laughed delightedly at the smells of seafood wafting up. Steamed lobster, crab cakes, soft shell crabs, and *paella* were unpacked. She inhaled the aromas, a hum of pleasure emanating from her. She turned to Harlan, a smile on her face which slowly faded as his expression turned to one of disgust.

"What's wrong? I thought you liked seafood!"

Harlan smiled weakly, "Me, too. But it's been so long, it just doesn't smell good to me."

"No problem," Randolph said. "I thought that might happen, so I brought this."

And from another bag, he produced a selection of containers. The smells coming from them were oddly familiar to Sarah. But Harlan broke into a huge smile and reached eagerly for them.

"Afghani food," Randolph whispered to her. "Since he's been away for such a long time, I thought he might take a while to get back to liking seafood. Smells and tastes a lot like Persian or Pakistani food."

"Oh! I was wondering why it smelled so familiar," she whispered back. "Good thinking!"

Randolph smiled at her and gave her a small bow.

They all settled down and for the next half-hour there was little talking, except for requests for refills and drinks. As each one finished, they settled back into their chairs.

Sarah got up from the table and brought back a tray with small glasses and two bottles.

"Cabernet Sauvignon and a ruby port. Choose your poison!" she said smiling. Harlan and Uncle Randolph chose the cabernet while Sarah and her father reached eagerly for the port.

Precisely at the stroke of seven, they heard footsteps on the stairs and a knock sounded on the door. Sarah went and opened it, waving Dr. Hotep into the room. She made the introductions.

"Dr. Hotep, my boyfriend, Harlan Willoughby, my father, Aaron Wilmarth, and Randolph Carter, a dear friend of the family that I fondly call my uncle," Randolph smiled at this. "Gentlemen, this is my dream therapist, Dr. Nayar Hotep."

Did she see for a moment a flash of startlement from the men's faces? Sarah wasn't sure.

"Hotep? Sounds Egyptian, I dare say," Uncle Randolph said casually.

Dr. Hotep smiled and waved vaguely, "Merely a professional name. My real name is Flagg, but that doesn't sound as good to my clients as 'Hotep.' Pardon the fiction, please."

"But you look African, at least your skin color," Randolph pursued.

Dr. Hotep laughed, "I've been told that many times. No, just an oddity of skin tone inherited from a far distant ancestor. You have no idea how difficult it has been in certain areas when attempting to earn a living! As you can see, there is no trace of African blood in my features. Sometimes, I wish I could go back and tell my ancestor to

176

not choose that partner. But since that is not possible, I just deal with it."

He turned to Sarah, "Will you show us your collection?"

She started. She'd almost forgotten why they were all there. Sarah decided on the dramatic route. She approached the dividing curtain, put a hand out to grab it, and intoned, "Gentlemen, the eerie collection of Sarah Wilmarth!"

With that, she swept the curtain aside.

Gasps came from all the men except Dr. Hotep. There were only five pieces and the covered bust. The first piece was a full figure of a man that appeared to be hunched over. On closer examination, they could see it was not a deformity but a result of the figure's normal bone structure. The face was oddly elongated with bulgy eyes and a flattened nose with slit nostrils. The fingers and toes were webbed and the whole thing looked like nothing so much as a humanoid frog. The nameplate read "Deep One."

The second was a figure of a bald woman that looked similar but more human than the Deep One, riding on the back of a leaping dolphin. The men looked more closely and could see an expression of delight on the woman's face. The nameplate simply said "Homecoming."

The third was what looked like a baby's cradle. In the swaddling clothes, nothing could be seen but a face that had thick lips, large pointy ears, and dark crinkly hair. The nameplate read "Wilbur Whateley at birth." Oddly, the figure looked more like a one-year old than a newborn. Dr. Hotep looked and nodded sagely while the other men whispered to each other.

The fourth was another full figure almost seven feet tall and quite handsome in the body. But the face! Instead of normal human features, there was an odd tentacle with eyes, mouths, and slits that one thought could be nostrils. Again, Dr. Hotep was interested and examined it closely. Under his breath, he muttered something. Sarah, who was closest, thought he said, "Surprisingly accurate!", although she wasn't sure. He looked at the name plate, which read "Naralep." A smile came to his face, and he clearly said, "Not quite."

The fifth figure was truly horrific. As Sarah had warned, it was only vaguely humanoid, being upright on two appendages. It looked vaguely crustacean but had many other paired appendages. The head was the worst! It was hard to tell if the head was more like an insect or a fungus shaped like an insect. There was no symmetry to the sense organs with eyes, nostrils, mouths, and tentacles placed randomly.

Again, Dr. Hotep just looked and nodded. The nameplate read "Mi-Go." Randolph and Harlan were startled, while Aaron looked away like he wanted nothing so much as to throw up. At that moment, a flash of lightning came through the windows followed immediately by a loud crash of thunder.

This startled everyone, even Dr. Hotep. And Sarah led them to the last piece, which was still covered by a large square of black velvet. The thrum of rain on the roof grew louder. She reached out and pulled off the cover. As they looked, another flash of lightning and peal of thunder sounded.

The bust showed a human head that bore vague resemblance to Harlan's but had what appeared to be masses of fungous growths all over it. The most revolting feature was the top of the head. It appeared as if the skull had been sawn off just above the eyes, and in place of a brain was a mass of odd protrusions and weird convolutions of something that bore no resemblance to human tissue.

Even more repulsive, the clay that Sarah had used had colors that were odd and revolting to the eyes. Aaron ran to the bathroom, from which the sound of vomiting could be heard. Harlan's face went white with shock and disgust and he cried out, "Destroy that thing!"

Dr. Hotep stepped in front of the piece, grabbing Harlan's arm, and deflecting his attempt to destroy it with a mallet.

"Control yourself, man! It's nothing but a sculpture."

Harlan looked at him and dropped the mallet. He turned and walked out of the room. Randolph and Dr. Hotep looked at the nameplate which simply read "Unknown." Sarah took the cloth and re-covered the bust.

"I don't think that one will ever be sold. I don't even know whether I'll destroy it or not."

Dr. Hotep said, "Don't make that choice now. You never know how you'll feel later, and it's easier to destroy or get rid of than to recreate."

Randolph agreed, "In spite of its horrific nature, it is easily one of the best pieces here. As a matter of fact, all these are excellent. If the rest of your sculptures were a match, it's no surprise you were able to sell them."

"Thank you, Uncle Randolph. I certainly intend to keep working on new pieces, so I hope you're right. Anyway, you've seen everything here, so let's call it a night."

So saying, she ushered them back to the living area and drew the curtain just as her father emerged from the bathroom. Sarah saw the expression of gratitude in his eyes.

"Would you like more wine? Or something stronger?" she asked.

"Stronger!" sounded three voices. Dr. Hotep, a small smile on his dace declined politely and said, "I've seen what I came to see. Thank you for a most illuminating experience, but I'll take my leave now. Enjoy your drinks, and I wish you pleasant dreams!"

He bowed and departed. Closing the door behind him, Sarah went back to her pantry, and took out a bottle from the bottom shelf. She set it on the table and turned to fetch four shot glasses from the cabinet above the stove.

"Tullamore Dew!" sounded her father's and uncle's voices in unison. "Capital selection, Sarah," her father continued as Randolph opened the bottle and poured healthy swigs for all four.

"I'll take my leave now, too," Harlan spoke up. "I have work I need to do and may have something very interesting to show you tomorrow evening."

He turned to Sarah and kissed her, then shook the hands of both men and left.

After one more shot, Aaron turned to Randolph and said, "Do you want to tell her?"

Randolph nodded.

"What?" Sarah asked.

"First, let me show you something, he said, fetching a book from the pocket of his coat. "Look at this."

He riffled through the pages and stopped, then put the book on the table, and turned it so she could see.

Sarah gasped. It was a picture, not a photograph, but an illustration of Dr. Hotep! But it didn't exactly resemble him, it seemed to be taller and more foreboding. There was a caption below it that said "A depiction of one of the avatars of Nyarlathotep."

"It looks rather like Dr. Hotep," Sarah said, perplexed. "But what does he have to do with this creature. Isn't he one of the Old Ones or something?"

"Not exactly, no," her father replied. "More like a servant of the Elder Gods. He is said to bring madness and death to humans, sometimes directly and other times through their dreams. We think he has somehow connected to you and Harlan through your dreams."

"But how? And why us?"

"We don't know that just yet. But here is why we think so."

Randolph took Dr. Hotep's card out of his pocket and laid it under the caption. Sarah was still confused.

Randolph looked at her with an expression of sympathy on his face. He took a pencil and pointed at the "N" on the card, then at the first letter in the name. Then he pointed to the L and to the letter "l" in the middle of the name. By that time, Sarah had realized what he was doing and could see the "Hotep" at the end of the name.

"But that seems to mean," her voice trailed off.

"That Dr. Hotep is actually Nyarlathotep? We think so, but we still have no way to prove it for certain. And there is no concrete evidence for him actually having direct interactions with humans other than old legends whose authenticity can't be verified. But we are concerned for you and Harlan! Has Harlan told you anything other than the story he told me? Or have you seen anything?"

Sarah thought for a moment, then remembered the odd prism she had seen on the desk in Harlan's hotel room.

"When I first got to the Derleth House and Harlan didn't answer the door, I opened it and saw him looking at something on the desk. He immediately threw a cloth over it and put it into a safe, but before he did, I saw what looked like a large prism."

"How large was it? Could you tell?" her father asked.

Sarah frowned in concentration as she thought about it, "I didn't see it for long, so I'm guessing it was about a foot long, with the sides being three inches. The strangest thing was the color. It looked similar to the colors I used for that last piece."

Aaron and Randolph looked at each other.

"Do you think?" Aaron started.

"The prism? I'm afraid it might be," Randolph replied.

"What did he find? Do you know what it is?" Sarah asked.

"We're not sure yet. Didn't he tell you? About getting hit in the head by something?"

Now Sarah was concerned. She told them about the falling piece of fungus that narrowly missed him, and how he had been hit in the head by something else.

"Did he say what it was?" her father asked.

"No. He did say he was going to see someone about it, but he didn't say who or when," Sarah's voice sounded apprehensive. "What do you think happened?"

Sarah was anxious about what had happened to Harlan. He had seemed a little odd, now that she thought about it.

She'd thought he would be happier to see her and had hoped that he would propose now that he had returned from his successful quest.

"Should I go with him to the doctor?"

"I don't think so. We need to do more research ourselves. And it doesn't seem he'd take kindly to our presence, or he would have already invited you," Randolph replied. "The best we can do now is check our sources. I'm afraid you'll just have to wait for now. As soon as we know anything, we'll be in touch."

"Sarah, dear, why don't you and Harlan come on the *Searcher* with me next week? You'll probably be glad for a chance to relax!"

Sarah smiled, "That sounds like a wonderful idea, Daddy! It's been too long since I sailed her!"

"Good! We'll set sail on Monday."

The two men took their leave. Sarah cleaned up and went to sleep.

Her sleep was broken by disturbing dreams but in the morning she remembered nothing of them. Just a vague sense of disquiet that stayed in the background of her thoughts.

After eating breakfast, she went into her studio and covered all the odd statuary with the canvas she used when she did unveilings at her shows, then started on a new piece. This was to be a dryad next to her tree.

When she stopped at lunch, she was pleased to see that it was coming along nicely with none of the disturbing elements that had been creeping in so often of late. She went back to work with a happiness that she now saw had been missing for weeks.

Mid-afternoon, her phone rang. It was Harlan!

"Harlan! How are you darling? What did the doctor say?"

"Doctor? Oh, no, I wasn't going to a doctor. Anyway, I've been too busy for that! I've got something that you need to see. Can you come by after supper?"

"Of course! What's wrong with your voice? You sound a little odd. Is there something in your room making a buzzing noise?"

"Buzzing? No. Oh, wait a minute," he said. She heard him put down his phone, then heard a click and a sound like clearing his throat. "Is that better?"

It was. He still sounded a bit odd, but the strange buzzing had stopped.

"Yes. Did you want to meet for supper again? Six o'clock? We could go for Italian."

"No. I have a bit more work to do. Come here at seven and everything will be ready."

"Alright," Sarah couldn't keep the disappointment out of her voice.

"I'm sorry, darling! I promise it will be something you will remember for the rest of your life."

"Oh! Yes, I'll be there at seven."

She hung up and went back to do more work. She'd hardly gotten started when her phone rang again. This time it was her father.

"How's my favorite daughter?" he asked.

She laughed at the old by-play.

"You mean your only daughter?"

"That's the one! Have you heard from Harlan yet?"

"Yes, I talked to him a little while ago. I think he's going to propose!"

"Really? That's great! What did he say?"

"He said it would be a night I'd remember for the rest of my life!"

There was a pause.

"Oh," Aaron said. "I hope you're right. So you're going over there?"

"Yes," Sarah was puzzled at the lack of excitement in her father's voice. She was sure that he liked Harlan, so what was the problem?

"I'm going there at seven."

"Excellent! Do you think we could meet you there?"

"I don't see why not. Shall we meet for dinner? Italian?"

"One moment," her father replied.

Sarah heard muffled sounds. Evidently, he was conferring with Uncle Randolph.

"Sure! The usual place?"

"Of course. Where else?"

They met at a local restaurant called D'Agostino's, and the food and company were excellent. Her father and uncle were subdued, but Sarah's happiness and joy infected them regardless. By the time supper was over, they, too, were smiling and joking.

When they arrived at the Derleth House and entered, the clerk recognized Sarah and called her over to the front desk.

"You going to see that guy in Room 666?"

When she replied in the affirmative, he said, "You'd better tell him to cut out whatever he's doing up there. I'm getting complaints from his neighbors about the loud weird sounds from his room. Any more complaints and I'll have to call the cops! And I don't like the looks of that weird guy who just went up there either."

That put a damper on their high spirits and they promised they would talk to him. When they got off the elevator and turned left, they understood the clerk's comments. They could hear strange voices coming from the room, one of them having buzzing overtones and the other, booming notes lower than a human voice could produce.

When Sarah knocked, the door swung open to her touch. The scene that greeted their eyes was so *outré* it didn't register at first. Dominating everything was a strange construction on the desk that centered around something that Randolph and Aaron realized was the prism Harlan had brought back from lost Leng. Standing in front of it was Harlan, dancing in a herky-jerky rhythm and chanting in an odd, buzzing voice that reminded her of the sound she'd heard when she'd talked to Harlan a few hours ago.

And standing a few feet away, arms raised and chanting in unison was Dr. Hotep, looking taller and blacker than they'd seen him yesterday.

But the climaxing horror was Harlan. The black turban was gone, and so was the top of his head! In its place was a pulsing, weirdly-shaped mass of fungous material whose nauseating color matched the odd colors of the prism. And he was turning toward her with a piece of that same fungous material in his hand.

"Put this on your head, then we will be as one," he said in that odd buzzing voice.

As Sarah's senses were overwhelmed by horror, she saw two things; the sight of Uncle Randolph pulling a revolver and putting a bullet through what had been

Harlan's brain and the Prism of Lost Leng, the other the sound of Dr. Hotep, who she now understood really was Nyarlathotep, shouting, "You fools!"

Two days later, Sarah stood on the deck of the *Searcher*, the blank look on her face showing that she was hardly aware her surroundings. Her father and uncle stood nearby, talking.

Aaron spoke first, "You really think this will help?"

Randolph snorted, "Don't sell your daughter short. She's young, healthy, and strong minded. The ocean voyage will clear her mind and restore her. I can relate. If I hadn't been expecting something like what we saw, I might have felt the same. As a matter of fact, I almost did anyway. And you weren't much better."

"You're right. Just one other thing. Remove or destroy those figures she showed us! We don't want anything in her studio that remotely resembles Cthulhu mythos figures!"

Randolph smiled, "Already in progress. Luckily, I was able to get that clerk at the Derleth House to hush things up, and nobody heard the shots."

Aaron raised his eyebrows, "How did you convince the clerk not to say anything?"

"Not very hard to do. He has a crush on Sarah, and I simply implied that she might be grateful when she came back to her senses. And who knows? She might. And it turns out that he is just finishing up his own studies at Miskatonic University, also in the art department; graphic design."

Aaron looked at his friend in surprise for a moment, then grinned, and clapped him on the back, "Always thinking! Sure you don't want to come with us?"

"No, I have other things to do. Just enjoy the sea and bring her back whole and complete! *Bon voyage*!"

Aaron saluted him and as Randolph went back down to the dock, he turned and started giving orders. Randolph watched the ship get underway. As it did, he saw a small smile appear on Sarah's face and she moved with increasingly firm steps to the bow of the *Searcher*, wind blowing her blonde hair back.

He smiled at that, then turned, and started back to his car. Randolph had his own ways of coping with such things and the main one was reporting to the White Council. He went back to the house, already composing the report in his mind.